Treasure of the
Templars

Other Five Star Titles
by Tim Champlin:

The Last Campaign
The Survivor
Deadly Season
Swift Thunder
Lincoln's Ransom
The Tombstone Conspiracy
Wayfaring Strangers

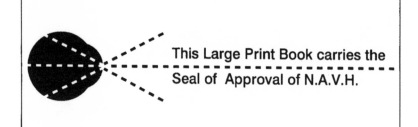

This Large Print Book carries the
Seal of Approval of N.A.V.H.

Treasure of the

Templars
A Western Story

TIM CHAMPLIN

Five Star
Unity, Maine

Five Star First Edition Western Series.

Published in 2000 in conjunction with
Golden West Literary Agency

The text of this edition is unabridged.

Set in 11 pt. Plantin by Al Chase.

Printed in the United States on permanent paper.

Library of Congress Cataloging-in-Publication Data

Champlin, Tim, 1937–
    Treasure of the Templars : a western story /
by Tim Champlin.
        p.   cm.
    "A Five Star western" — T.p. verso.
    ISBN 0-7862-2121-6 (hc : alk. paper)
    1. Treasure-trove — Fiction. I. Title.
PS3553.H265 T74 2000
    813´.54—dc21
                                                        00-044279

For
Jon Tuska and Vicki Piekarski
who saved my writing career

Prologue

Scotland
August, 1897

Professor Roddy McGinnis's heart was pounding and his mouth dry as he squatted on his heels in the rubble of the medieval dungeon. Using a sheath knife, he'd finally worked loose from the wall in front of him a wedge-shaped stone the size of his head. A tiny, V-shaped notch filed into the edge of the stone had piqued his curiosity. Shafts of dusty sunlight, lancing through the roofless castle ruin overhead, revealed an oblong object in the space behind the stone. He removed a packet bound in oilcloth, shook the dirt off, and unwrapped it. A musty book fell out. With trembling hands, he opened the cracked, leather binding. The yellowed pages were filled with closely spaced lines of a fine, flowing script. Even in good light, the writing was hard to decipher. But it was in English, albeit Elizabethan English. Just inside the front cover, the name **PETER STIRLING** was written in bold letters.

"By the mines of King Solomon!" he breathed. He looked toward the four students he was supervising on this dig. They were all busy excavating at the far end of the trench along the dungeon wall. Trying to calm his excitement, he turned his back to them and put on his wire-rimmed glasses.

Peter Stirling was a 16th-Century Scottish knight who'd succumbed to fever in this very castle more than three hundred years ago. He'd been imprisoned and tortured on the orders of his superiors in the Knights Templar, a disbanded order of warrior monks. Stirling was the only surviving member of a small party of knights who had allegedly transported the gold treasury of the order to a safer hiding place in the New World. The rumor had come down the centuries that Stirling, returning alone to Scotland after a harrowing two-year trip to America, had been refused a reward of lands and title in Scotland. In turn, he'd refused to tell the Grand Master the exact whereabouts of the treasure that he and his deceased companions had hidden. For this, he'd been jailed and tortured for weeks until he eventually died. But his secret had died with him.

For the past three hundred and fifty years, members of the Templars, now a shadow organization, had searched in vain for the treasure. Over time, the golden hoard had taken on the legendary status of a lost mine or the buried treasure of Captain Kidd. It had become part of folklore and, like the Holy Grail, or the True Cross, it was an entertaining legend. But almost none of McGinnis's colleagues in the field of archaeology even believed in the existence of the vast treasure trove.

McGinnis carefully leafed through the book that appeared to be the personal journal of Peter Stirling. He swallowed hard. If this was genuine, he had just stumbled onto the discovery of a lifetime. He would have to examine it at length, but at first glance the ancient volume did not appear to be a fraud. At worst, if the journal revealed nothing of Stirling's trip to the New World with the treasure, the book would still be a valuable historical artifact that could fund at least two more expeditions to the Near East for his university.

Yet, as he looked at the dated entries, he realized they coincided with the years Stirling was said to have made his voyage to the Gulf Coast of North America. Why had the book been secreted behind this loose stone in Stirling's dungeon? Wouldn't his captors have found and confiscated it? Stirling had no relatives except a wife he married after his return. Had she smuggled it to him? For what purpose? Perhaps so he could continue to make entries, documenting and denouncing his unjust tormentors during the weeks of his imprisonment. The book itself might give the answers when he examined it in his hotel room later. He saw no need to share this find with his students.

He wrapped the rotting cloth around the book and slipped it inside his canvas shirt. It might take several days, or even weeks, to decipher and transcribe the contents. But a thrill went over him at the thought that, lying inside his shirt, could well be the key that would unlock one of history's greatest mysteries.

Chapter One

Central Kentucky
April, 1898

Marcus Flood caught his breath and stopped still in the dusty Kentucky road. Thirty yards ahead was one of the strangest sights he'd ever seen—a white-haired man in a buggy being accosted by two armored horsemen. The morning sun glinted off the cylindrical metal helmets that covered their heads and necks. And each man wore a hauberk—a coat of chain mail reaching past the hips. Flood had the oddest feeling he'd just rounded a turn and stepped back into medieval Europe. But, instead of swords or maces, these men were armed with modern revolvers.

The horsemen were facing away from him at a slight angle, their voices muffled by the helmets and distance. Flood was certain the slim, hatless, white-haired man in the buggy had seen him, but the victim made no sign. Flood quietly stepped back a few paces until he was beyond the cover of a clump of small cedar trees bordering the road. Heart pounding, he lowered the canvas traveling bag from his shoulder. His mind was in a sudden whirl. What was going on here—some sort of practical joke? He was afoot and unarmed. Should he interfere? The old man had not cried out for help. If this was a real robbery, there was little he could do to help, and he might very well get himself shot. But if he did nothing, they might gun down the hapless old man. He tried to salve his conscience and his fear by telling himself that, if he stayed out of sight, the highwaymen would only take the man's valuables and ride off, doing their victim no physical harm. But he couldn't be sure of this. Then, again, the old man might try to make some foolish resistance.

Whatever he decided, it would have to be quick. He took his bag and crept off the road among the stunted cedars. The trees had taken root in a thin layer of soil that overlay some ledges of limestone. The flat rock thrust out of the ground here and there, and some broken pieces lay about. Keeping one eye on the confrontation through the evergreen branches, he quickly selected a half-dozen fist-sized rocks with good heft. He stuffed two into each side pocket of his corduroy coat, and retained one in each hand, flexing his arms.

As he cautiously crept forward, arms up to fend off the prickly branches, he could see the drama on the road beginning to play out. The man on the buggy seat was yelling something and gesticulating wildly. One of the chain-mail-clad horsemen suddenly swung up a long lance from the far side of his mount. Before Flood could move, the helmeted rider kicked his horse, and the animal lunged forward. For one eternal second, Flood saw the broad lance point poised three feet from the old man's chest. Then, in a blink, the old man vanished, and the lance buried itself in the back of the buggy seat. The long spear splintered, and the unchecked momentum flung the rider forward over his horse's neck, and he tumbled onto the buggy's near wheel.

Even as Flood cocked his arm and aimed the rock, he heard a high-pitched yell as the old man bobbed up from behind the dashboard of the buggy. Flood's arm snapped forward in a powerful overhand throw. The missile whistled toward its target—the second robber—who was aiming his pistol at the old man.

The rock *whanged* off the back of the helmet at the same instant the pistol exploded. The man reeled in his saddle.

Before either of the horsemen could recover and realize he was under attack, Flood unleashed the other five rocks he was carrying. Three of them found the men, and two of the sharp missiles hit the flanks of their horses, causing the animals to snort and plunge out of control. The dappled gray hitched to the buggy was also tossing its head and trying to sidle away from the commotion, while the lancer who'd fallen was struggling to get hold of his spooked horse and remount.

As the distracted robbers were trying to get a shot off at Flood, the old man whipped his horse. The light buggy jumped forward and came tearing past Flood, bouncing and skidding around the bend as the panicked animal hit full gallop.

One of the robbers finally got his mount under control and got off a hurried shot at Flood who was scrambling for cover. His element of surprise was gone. The bullet plowed up dirt three feet short of his foot as he leaped back into the trees and threw himself on the ground behind his canvas bag. Another slug thudded into the duffel.

Flood said a quick mental prayer, knowing he was helpless before these two. He could see nothing of the face behind the eye slits in the helmet, but the man was wearing a sleeveless white tunic over his hauberk, with a large red cross emblazoned on the chest. Suddenly the second man yelled something at the one who was firing. He flung down the splintered haft of the lance and leaped down to snatch a small, black leather case from the ground. Then he swung back into the saddle, and both horsemen whirled their mounts away, thundering off up the road.

Panting with fear and exertion, Flood watched as they

grew smaller in the distance, dust spurting from the hoofs until they disappeared over a rise. Flood rubbed his eyes and stepped out into the road, looking after them and already beginning to doubt what he had just seen and experienced. The drumming of the hoof beats faded, and the only sign that anyone else had been there was the thin veil of dust hanging in the cool air. His ragged breathing began to steady as he looked around, trying to comprehend the suddenly vanished vision, trying to remember if he had eaten some bad food the night before at the monastery. Brother Anthanasius had made mushroom gravy from wild morels he'd picked in the woods. Maybe he'd accidentally gotten hold of some hallucinatory mushrooms. Surely he couldn't have just witnessed two men in 12th-Century armor accosting an old man in a buggy on a Kentucky back road. It simply couldn't be. After all, this was a sunny April morning in 1898—not 1298.

He turned to look back down the road the other way. There was no sign of the buggy. The only evidence that this scene had even taken place were the scuff marks in the dirt of the roadway, the splintered haft of a lance, and a bullet hole in the canvas duffel bag he'd retrieved and flung onto his shoulder.

"Damnedest thing," he muttered aloud, just to hear the reassurance of his own voice. "Maybe I'm losing touch. Too much research into the Middle Ages . . . like Don Quixote. But somebody *was* here." He put a forefinger into the bullet hole in his bag. "But I'd best keep my mouth shut about this."

He surveyed the deserted green fields and woods around him. Except for the sharp, cheerful trill of a meadowlark, everything was as quiet and deserted as when he'd started out from the monastery at sunrise, two hours ago. He had no particular destination in mind, but also no desire to continue in the direction of the departed horsemen. He reversed his course and started walking back down the road after the vanished buggy. After all, the small town of New Haven lay that way. And by the time he reached it, it would be nearly lunch time. He had just enough money for about two meals. Then his worldly wealth would be reduced to one change of clothing, a blanket, and a few small books he carried in his bag. There were trains in New Haven—trains that ran in and out in all directions. Perhaps he could slip aboard a southbound freight toward his parents' home in Nashville, more than a hundred miles away. He didn't particularly want to go back there but, at the moment, could think of nowhere else to go. After a year and a half as a lay brother in the Trappist monastery at Gethsemani, he'd agonized over the decision to leave. But he'd concluded the silent life was not for him. He tried to view this as a positive choice, and not another failure. But he had a gnawing feeling that, at age thirty-five, each new beginning was only a fresh mistake.

He'd found nothing so far that satisfied him. He'd dropped out of college at age nineteen to enlist in the cavalry. But the four-year adventure had proven to be mostly hard work and frustration, serving in New Mexico Territory from 1881 to 1885. It was stable duty, sentry duty, and monotonous drill interspersed with endless, exhausting mounted patrols in pursuit of Apaches who vanished into the vast landscape like smoke. After shedding his cavalry blue, he'd returned to Tennessee and a series of unfulfilling jobs as a government clerk, freight handler for the railroad, even a brief stint as a gun salesman, while, in his spare time, pitching for a local baseball team.

He trudged ahead, lost in thought and hardly conscious of nature awakening around him. A short time later he passed a farmer driving a wagon with a span of mules. He opened his mouth to ask if the man had seen a black buggy with a white-haired driver, but the hard look on the man's face deterred him. Flood merely waved and walked on. A year of fasting, work, and prayer among sixty of his brother monks was powerful medicine. The habit of silence had convinced him that most conversation was frivolous.

Another half hour of walking brought him again within sight of the monastery church spire above the greening spring trees. The tall stone building was a quiet, solid symbol of stability that had stood there in the Kentucky woods for more than thirty years. Before he reached the monastery gates, he turned to follow the road that bent toward the west. He swallowed a lump in his throat as he thought of what the monks would be doing about now. Some of the brothers would be in the fields, a couple of them would be baking bread, two or three more preparing the sparse noon meal, some possibly clearing brush and planting trees, or studying in the library, writing, chanting tierce in the dark, wooden stalls of the Gothic church. It was a quiet, orderly life that he was already beginning to miss. But a man had to have his basic priorities straight in order to live this life. His faith in God remained strong, but, while studying and researching, he'd reached the point where his unquestioning belief in the traditions of the Church and some of its leaders, past and present, had been seriously shaken. Somehow these questions had to be resolved. And, of course, there were so many young women waiting out there in the world. . . .

Flood reflected that being extraordinarily handsome had been much more of a curse to him than a blessing. Good looks and good health were two things he'd always taken for granted, with no trace of pride, since he couldn't claim credit for either. Certainly his attractiveness to women, coupled with his own weakness of will, had caused him untold heartbreak and grief over the years. *Monday's child is fair of face;*

Tuesday's child is full of grace; Wednesday's child is full of woe . . .—the old rhyme ran through his head. By birth, he was Monday's child, but he fit the description of Wednesday's child as well.

His anguish cast a pall over the beautiful April morning as he trudged along. Within a mile he came upon the buggy. It was off the road, and the right front wheel was shattered against a stump. The dappled gray had been unhitched and was tied to a sapling, apparently unhurt. Flood approached cautiously, looking for the driver, but saw no sign of the old man. He laid a hand on the broken lance that still protruded from the padded leather seat back. Here was further proof it hadn't been an hallucination. He examined the lathered animal, and could detect no obvious injury.

"Get away from my horse!" A lean figure bounded out of a clump of blackberry bushes, arms waving and white hair flying.

Flood fell back a few steps, his heart leaping at the sudden apparition.

"Where are they? Did you see them? Are they gone?" The questions came rattling out like the staccato hammering of a woodpecker. The old man's sharp nose seemed to be sniffing for danger as his quick blue eyes darted here and there.

"They're gone. Rode off north," Flood replied.

"By the bones of Bede!" the old man cried. "Foxed 'em again. They're not too smart. But they're persistent. As soon as they find out there's nothing in that case they don't already know, they'll be hot on my trail. I've got to get a move on."

"You dropped that leather case on purpose?"

A sly look crept over the old man's face. "Won't slow 'em down for long. You know, if they've been around for seven centuries, they won't quit now. Especially since I know. . . ."

17

He paused and looked suspiciously at Flood. "Say, who are you, anyway?"

"I'm the one who just saved your hide back there. And you're most welcome, I'm sure," he added sarcastically as he sidled away, keeping a wary eye on this strange character. "They could have killed us both, if they'd really wanted to. Why didn't they? What were they after?"

"I . . . can't really say. Here, look at this buggy. You think you can fix this wheel so I can drive on?"

Flood glanced at the broken spokes. "Not a chance. Although . . . we could probably switch one of the rear wheels to the front and fashion some sort of skid for the back. It'll create more drag for the horse, but it might work long enough to get you into New Haven."

"Let's get to it, then!" The old man rubbed his hands gleefully.

Flood began to wonder if this man were a refugee from some asylum. Maybe, if he didn't press him, he could get some more information. "By the way, my name's Marc Flood," he said easily, offering his hand.

A look of suspicion quickly overcame the man's sharp features. But he finally said: "I'm Roddy McGinnis, a professor from the University of Chicago."

And I'm the Pope, Flood thought. When McGinnis didn't offer to shake, Flood dropped his hand.

Working quickly, the two of them wrenched the buggy off the stump onto the road, jacked it up, and removed both right side wheels, placing the good rear wheel on the front. Then they were able to split off two fair-size, springy limbs from some nearby trees. Bending them under and over the rear axle, they managed to fashion a very crude skid. The buggy sagged to within a foot of the ground at the right rear, but it was the best they could do. They re-hitched the gray.

Except for brief comments related to the task, no conversation passed between the two while they worked. Flood was convinced this man was some sort of lunatic who would require very careful handling. The only shade of doubt was the memory of the armor-clad robbers. They had been real. McGinnis—if that was his name—had not imagined them.

Something over an half hour was consumed by this work. Finally Flood stepped back and surveyed their efforts. "There. That should see you into town. New Haven's only a couple miles ahead. I don't know of a wheelwright there, but there's a good blacksmith who can probably fix that for you."

McGinnis looked at him with narrowed blue eyes. "You're a good lad, Flood."

Maybe McGinnis had been drunk and was just sobering up, Flood thought, since he was now beginning to act somewhat normal. But he had not smelled any liquor on the old man. Nor had he seen any bottle or jug in the buggy. And if McGinnis had traveled all the way from Chicago, he carried no coat, hat, or change of clothes. Flood decided to make another stab at satisfying his curiosity. "Did you know those robbers?"

"Not personally," McGinnis replied carefully.

Flood noticed that, even though McGinnis's thick hair was completely white, his smooth-shaven face was unlined and very youthful. And the man's physical energy certainly belied any great accumulation of years.

"Where did they come from?"

McGinnis chewed his lower lip and looked away without replying. At last he said: "I've been delayed here too long. They'll be back. Maybe I should go back to the monastery."

"Why?"

"That's where I was going when they caught up with me. They'll at least respect sanctuary."

Flood's impatience was rising again at McGinnis's habit of not answering direct questions. "I think I've helped you enough today to deserve an explanation."

For the first time, Flood felt the older man really studying him. "Do you live around here?"

"I just left the monastery. Been a brother there for over a year."

"Where are you going now?" The small, blue eyes bored into him.

"Not sure. Possibly to Nashville, where my parents live, until I can get a job." He felt foolish admitting this, even to a stranger.

"Laddy, I'll give you a job, if you're interested."

"Doing what?" Broke as he was, Flood was still cautious, having no wish to get involved with this eccentric individual. The man could be dangerous. The wrong word might set him off.

"As my traveling companion and bodyguard until we reach Nashville. Do you have a gun?"

"If I did, I'd have used it back there."

"We can buy you one in New Haven. As it happens, I'm going to Nashville myself."

Flood didn't believe this for a moment.

Apparently McGinnis read the doubt on Flood's face. "In spite of what you're thinking, young man, it is true, and you might just be my means of getting there safely. I am to deliver a paper at Vanderbilt University before a meeting of the ISHA."

"The what?"

"The International Society of Historical Anthropologists."

"Well, I suppose it wouldn't hurt to travel together that far," Flood said slowly.

"It would save me from having to seek sanctuary in the monastery."

Flood nodded, thinking what turmoil this man might cause in the quiet, orderly life of the monks, although the tough little French abbot, Father Benedict Dupont, was accustomed to dealing with strange visitors.

"Were all your papers in your case?"

"Not all of them." He winked conspiratorially. "Got 'em stashed under the buggy seat."

Flood nodded, wondering but not asking.

"So now you know. You could overpower me and steal them, if you've a mind to, but I'm a good judge of human nature. And I believe you to be trustworthy."

Flood nodded again. McGinnis was definitely a little off plumb. Yet, traveling with him might provide a way home—if they weren't attacked again. And he had to eat. Lack of funds was the driving force in his decision to accept. But it was not without a stab of anguish. Compromise was again part of his life. Would Christ have turned the other cheek to those armored bandits—given them His coat as well as His shirt? Flood's own ambivalence about war and violent conflict had been the primary cause of his leaving the monastery.

"My niece is to meet me in Nashville in two days," McGinnis continued. "So we'd best get on."

"You ride and I'll walk to keep some of the weight off that skid," Flood said. "That thing won't stand another hundred and sixty pounds."

"No. Get in. We need to make some time. Those men will be after me before the day is much older. By the blood of the martyrs, they'll finish me next time!"

"What do your friends call you? Professor Roddy McGinnis?"

"Either Mac or Roddy."

Flood reached into the buggy and ripped the iron spear point out of the leather seat. "Then, let's get to town, Mac," he said, holding it up. "If this is what I'm going to be dealing with, I want to do it on my own terms."

Chapter Two

Nashville, Tennessee
Late April, 1898

Merliss McGinnis stepped off the trolley car and took two steps toward the curb when her heel slipped down between two wet cobblestones and she gasped as she turned her ankle. She caught her balance and limped to the sidewalk, clenching her teeth as the electric trolley clattered away along West End Avenue.

Suddenly a strong arm was supporting her, and she was startled to hear a mellow voice say: "Are you all right, Miss McGinnis?"

"I . . . I'm fine," she stammered, trying to extricate herself from the encircling arm of this stranger. He was about six feet tall, wore a brown suit, bowler hat, and sported a small mustache. "How did you know my name?"

He let go of her and touched the brim of his hat. "Robert Anderson," he said, smiling. "I'm attending the ISHA conference, just as you are," he said, taking her arm and watching for an opening in the wagon and buggy traffic to guide her across the thoroughfare to the red brick Vanderbilt University campus. "I was sent to meet you," he continued. "The chancellor's secretary told me you were rooming in town and would be out this morning. A telephone call came for you."

"A telephone call?"

"The chancellor has a telephone in his office. I think the call was from your uncle."

"Not bad news?" She was suddenly apprehensive.

"I don't think so. Most people send bad news by telegram. The secretary will give you the message, but she mentioned something about your uncle being delayed."

"I hope he won't miss the scheduled time for his lecture."

"I believe he's on the program for one o'clock tomorrow afternoon," Anderson offered.

"Is this the main administration building?" she inquired. This was only her second visit to Nashville, and she wasn't familiar with the Vanderbilt campus.

"Yes, but the chancellor's office is in the third building over there." He pointed ahead. "You know, it won't be long until every office and every home will have a telephone."

She hardly heard what Anderson was saying as she tried to guess what message she would receive. Had her uncle met with some kind of accident on his drive down from Chicago? She'd tried to convince him to take the train, but he was too stubborn or independent and—she had to admit it—just plain eccentric. For some reason, he wanted to make the drive himself, with his own black buggy and dappled gray gelding. He'd written her that it was spring, and he didn't want to be cooped up in some smoky day coach for five hundred miles. Besides, he'd argued, he wanted to have his own conveyance for both of them to get around town after he arrived. She thought how she'd been looking forward to this Easter break from her teaching job at a private school in New Orleans. Now, she worried, something had happened that might interfere with these plans. Anderson led her up the stone steps of a building and opened the door for her. They went down the hall, and he opened another door.

She stepped inside and saw nothing but a bed, a small

table, and two chairs. This looked like a dormitory room.

"What . . . ?"

Just as she turned, he locked a muscular arm around her shoulders and clamped the other hand over her mouth. Her stomach muscles contracted in sudden fear. At five foot, six, she had a willowy, athletic build, but was no match in size and strength for this man. She was suddenly terrified that she was about to be raped, and gathered her strength to fight.

He dragged her to the bed and flung her down. She took a deep breath, but the scream died in her throat as he suddenly produced a pistol from under his coat. "Don't make a sound!" he hissed.

She gasped, staring at the black muzzle two feet from her and felt the blood draining from her face. "I don't have much money, if that's what you want," she wavered, secretly hoping this was robbery and not rape. If she hadn't been sitting on the bed, she thought her weak knees probably wouldn't have held her up.

As if reading her mind, he chuckled: "I don't want your money, and I don't want your body . . . although that wouldn't be at all bad."

She felt the blood surging back into her face. She'd grown up in Chicago with only her uncle as guardian. Lacking the female counsel of a mother or older sister, she'd still learned to fend for herself and deal with boys and young men at an early age. Very few of them really alarmed her. This one did.

"No, you are only a pawn in a much larger game. You're our insurance that your uncle will provide us with his notes and won't give that lecture tomorrow."

"Then there was no phone call?"

"No."

"What do you plan to do with me?"

"Hold you here until Professor McGinnis arrives. Once

we have him in our hands, you will be released."

She knew her uncle was a respected full professor and had studied in Europe. As a well-to-do bachelor, he'd been made her legal guardian some twenty years before when she was only five years old after her parents perished in the great Chicago fire. Even after she was grown, she'd remained close to her Uncle Mac, as he preferred to be called, since he was the only parent she'd known. And he treated her like the daughter he had never had. Although not an archaeology major, she'd accompanied him on two summer digs to the Near East during her first two years as a University of Chicago student. Instead of the thrilling adventure she half expected, she'd found those trips mostly hot, dirty work. But she knew little of his academic life and research, other than the reputation he seemed to have among his fellow scholars. She wondered if her abduction had something to do with professional jealousy, although she couldn't imagine anything this violent resulting from the study of history and the digging up of old bones and castles.

"Why do you want him?" she finally asked, as Anderson straddled one of the straight, wooden chairs, holding his gun loosely.

"That's no concern of yours. The less you know, the better chance you'll have of being let go alive."

She swallowed her fear, hoping her face didn't show her terror. At the same time, her mind could hardly grasp the reality of this situation. She felt as if she were in shock. It sounded as if this were much more than some sort of professional academic jealousy. Had her eccentric uncle somehow gotten himself into serious debt to ruthless loan sharks or big-time gamblers? He frequently traveled out of the country. Maybe he was involved in smuggling. What else could it be? She had no clue.

"What do you expect me to do until he arrives? It may not be until tomorrow morning," she stated with some heat, beginning to recover her composure.

"You'll stay right here in this room until then. There's a chamber pot under that bed, and a friend of mine will bring some food shortly. If McGinnis arrives on time, you should be free to go in less than twenty-four hours."

Her eyes wandered to the window behind her. She also noted that Anderson had not locked the door.

"If you're getting any ideas about trying to escape, forget them," Anderson said, apparently reading her glances. "You'd only get yourself hurt, or worse." He gave her a tight smile, then pulled a folded copy of *The Nashville American* newspaper from his coat pocket and tossed it onto the bed. "Here's something to pass the time. Relax. You'll be here a while."

She dropped her eyes submissively, but her mind was racing, trying to think of some way out of this mess. She had to get away, had to intercept and warn her uncle. It would be a lot better if she knew what this was all about. If this man and his friends couldn't get their hands on Roddy McGinnis, she would be used for ransom until he surrendered to them. What had started out as a bright spring day had suddenly turned dark and ugly.

The sun streaming through the window fell on the newspaper, and she picked it up, noting that the press was still whipping up the public for a war with Spain. It had been almost three months since the sinking of the battleship *Maine* in Havana harbor, but the cry for war was still being trumpeted from the front pages. Troops were assembling from all over the country to train in a camp near San Antonio, Texas.

She dropped the paper and stared out the window at the

stately oaks and maples and the flowering dogwoods. She fervently wished she were in Texas, or somewhere else far away from here, she and her uncle, safe from all this. But where was Uncle Mac now?

Chapter Three

New Haven, Kentucky

"By the boots of Saint Crispin! Is that bumbling blacksmith ever going to finish fixing that wheel?" Roddy McGinnis growled as he paced nervously in front of the open-sided smithy.

"Not so loud," Flood whispered, jerking his head toward the hairy, muscular man in the leather apron working just inside. A wooden hammer thudded against the wheel hub. "I think he's almost done." The professor's oath finally penetrated Flood's consciousness. "By the way, who is Saint Crispin? Or did you just make that up?"

McGinnis stopped pacing and looked up in surprise. "Of course not. He's the patron saint of shoemakers."

Flood shook his head, wondering at this man. He turned away and slipped a hand inside his corduroy coat to the butt of a Colt revolver tucked into a shoulder holster. He hadn't gotten used to the weight and bulk of it yet, but felt much more secure with the weapon handy. After leaving the buggy wheel for repairs, their first task in town had been to purchase a gun at the hardware store. McGinnis had let him pick the weapon he wanted and then paid for it. As Flood was selecting the gleaming blue-black Colt Bisley model, with black, hard rubber grips, the irony of his situation was not lost on him. In one day he'd gone from a poor Trappist monk to an armed bodyguard.

They ate at a nearby café and spent the remainder of the day in the second-floor room of a brick hotel. From here they could view the main street below, but there was no sign of the men who'd attacked. Flood knew that watching for pursuit was a futile exercise; those men were not likely to ride into town wearing that ridiculous medieval armor. And he'd been too busy during the attack to pay attention to their horses. He vaguely remembered them as being dark, as were the vast majority of horses he'd ever seen.

In spite of his apprehension, Flood slept soundly, wrapped in his blanket on the floor near the professor's bed, loaded gun near his hand.

Professor McGinnis had a change of clothing under the buggy seat along with a thick sheaf of papers. While they waited for the stolid blacksmith to finish other work before he could get to their wheel, the professor spent the afternoon and evening in the hotel room studying the papers and scribbling notes.

"There ya go, gents. Good as new." The blacksmith rolled the wheel out to them. "Jack up that buggy and I'll put 'er on."

Twenty minutes later the wheel was installed, the blacksmith paid, and they were on their way. As the sun climbed and the weather warmed, they stopped to fold back the canvas buggy top.

In spite of Flood's nervous watchfulness, the day passed peacefully while they wound southward. Here and there farmers were plowing their fields with mules for spring planting after two weeks of off and on rain.

About an hour after noon they stopped by a ford in the shade of a large cottonwood to water and rest the horse and to eat the sandwiches they had bought at a café in New Haven that morning. They ate with little conversation, Flood deciding this was not the time to press McGinnis for information about who and why someone would want to rob or kill him. As long as he was getting food and transportation in addition to cash at the end of the journey to Nashville, he could afford to hold his curiosity at bay. As he walked away from the buggy, munching his sandwich and watching the clear little stream gurgle over some rock ledges, he thought that it would make his job easier if he had some idea what to expect from any would-be assassins. He might be able to anticipate what was coming next. But this strange professor had so far chosen not to confide in him.

Nearly an hour later they climbed back in, and McGinnis drove on. They passed two horsemen going in the opposite direction, and Flood kept his hand on his gun until they rode by. Two hours later they overtook a farmer hauling a wagonload of manure. The weathered farmer raised his hand in greeting as they went around him.

Late in the afternoon, Flood estimated they were approaching the Tennessee border. The countryside was mostly wooded, except where the hardwood forests had been cleared over the past half century to provide fields for crops and pasture. McGinnis had chosen to keep to the back roads, so they passed through no towns. Only now and then did they spot a few rude log or clapboard buildings of a farmstead, or see a wire fence enclosing a few cattle on new grass.

Flood offered to spell the older man at the reins, but McGinnis shook his head. "By the beard of Saint Olaf, I'm paying you to guard me. If that isn't enough to keep you busy, maybe we should part company." He considered Flood with a bright-eyed, quizzical look.

Flood, for the life of him, could not figure out if the professor was joking or serious. The blue eyes, the sharp features, quick movements, and sarcastic manner brought to

31

mind the Irish Little People that Flood had seen depicted in books. Yet the lean man didn't seem concerned about his life being in danger. He sang softly to himself as he drove along, seemingly lost in thought.

Flood reflected that this trip might turn out to be the easiest he'd ever made, as the day wore down and the sun slid behind the trees. He began to wonder if McGinnis planned to camp out for the night or had some town with a hotel in mind. It didn't matter to Flood, except that they had nothing to eat. If they got an early start tomorrow, he estimated they'd be in Nashville before noon.

While he was distracted by this speculation, they were passing along a solid wall of hardwood forest on one side of the road and an open field on the other. Flood thought he caught a slight movement out of the corner of his eye in the woods to his right. If it were a deer, it had faded into the thick woods when he turned to look. A minute later he heard a *thump* that seemed to come from the back of the buggy. Had a back wheel run over something? He hadn't felt them jolt over a rock or rut.

Suddenly he heard a hissing noise, saw a reflected white light, and felt heat on the back of his neck. He twisted around. With a blinding flash, the entire rear of the buggy, including the folded canvas top, was engulfed in flames. A yell burst from his lips, and he fell off the seat, his back slamming against the dashboard.

McGinnis whipped the gray into a gallop. Flood automatically drew his gun and was scanning the woods for any sign of their attackers. For several long seconds he saw nothing. Then the feathered shaft of a short, crossbow arrow appeared, as if by magic, in the wooden dashboard beside him and burst into flames. He cringed away from the fire, and began firing blindly at whatever was attacking them from the rear. But the clouds of dust billowing up from their wheels and the soft roar of flames being fanned backward by their speed blocked his view of anything behind.

They hit some deep ruts that grabbed the front wheels, nearly throwing the wildly careening buggy out of control. The two men were flung from side to side on the seat as the buggy slewed. It was obvious there was no way they could save the buggy short of running it into a river or pond, and there was no water anywhere about.

Flood was sure at least two horsemen were after them. It would be only a matter of seconds before he and McGinnis would have to jump to keep from being burned alive. And they would leap right into the path of the oncoming attackers.

"We have to jump!" Flood yelled.

McGinnis didn't reply. He didn't look back or at Flood; he kept his attention fixed on the running gray. The powerful horse was thundering down the narrow dirt road. McGinnis, white hair flying in the wind, was whipping him to greater speed.

Pieces of the canvas top began to burn off and fly away, and the men had to twist sideways to avoid the flames licking out from the burning wooden dashboard in front of them.

"Slow down and get ready to jump!" Flood yelled again. The flames and dust cloud still screened everything behind them, and no horsemen had come up alongside on the narrow road.

McGinnis still ignored him. At first, Flood thought the old man didn't want to lose his horse. But, finally, McGinnis yelled back: "I can't jump. I'll lose all my papers!"

"What?"

"In a pouch under the seat!"

"Get 'em!"

McGinnis handed Flood the reins, and the two of them

slid to their knees as the professor lifted the hinged seat. He thrust an arm inside and dragged out a foot-long leather pouch fastened with straps. The dappled gray thundered ahead, wearing blinders and apparently not yet aware of the inferno chasing him.

"Is there a linchpin on this buggy?"

McGinnis yanked up a section of the floorboard and pointed at a ring on the undercarriage. "If I yank that out, the horse and shafts go!"

Flood eased the gray back to a canter. The heat was becoming intense. He took a quick glance over his shoulder. A helmeted attacker was urging his straining horse alongside.

"On the count of three, yank that pin and we both jump toward the woods!" Flood shouted.

McGinnis pumped his head vigorously that he understood.

"One! Two! *Three!*"

Flood threw the reins as McGinnis's hand came up with the pin, and the next second both men were flying off the side of the open buggy, away from the oncoming horseman. The professor's shoe clipped Flood's head as they hit and rolled in a tangle of arms and legs. The front wheels hit a bump, crimped sideways, and the buggy catapulted into the air, flaming débris flying in all directions. The gray continued down the road, dragging the shafts he was still harnessed to. In the few seconds it took Flood to roll over in the weeds and look up, he saw one of the attackers who was following too closely, go down, his horse's legs kicking in the air as the animal fell on top of its rider.

The other man had managed to rein up and was now whirling his mount toward Flood and McGinnis as they lay in the brush of the sloping bank on the edge of the woods. He came charging toward them, raising a crossbow to his shoulder. The bolt shot forward and buried itself in the ground inches from Flood who was rolling onto his back, Colt in hand. He fired upward and had the satisfaction of seeing a groove appear alongside the gleaming helmet. The rider reeled in his saddle, and Flood fired again, striking him in the shoulder. The horseman nearly fell.

McGinnis jumped up, yelling, and getting in the way as he staggered toward the shelter of the trees. The wounded horseman dropped the reins, and his mount went snorting and lunging back up onto the road.

Just then, the other attacker, who had lost his helmet when his horse crashed into the burning buggy, leveled a pistol at Flood. Flood never heard the shot, but saw a dart of flame from the barrel and felt the bullet burn past his left cheek. Lying flat, he fired almost simultaneously, but missed.

The armored man afoot caught the wounded attacker's horse and vaulted onto the animal's back, behind the saddle. With one wild shot over his shoulder, he kicked the horse in the flanks, and the two men, riding double, galloped away down the road.

Flood got to his hands and knees, his Colt cocked and ready. But the two were gone. He'd gotten a quick look at one of the attackers—shaggy black hair and a thick black mustache on a man close to six feet tall. The face was fixed in his memory; he wanted to be sure he could identify his assailant if he ever saw him again.

His breath was coming in gasps. "Mac, come on out. They're gone!" he yelled over his shoulder. The broken buggy still burned in a heap across the road about twenty yards away where it had set fire to some dead grass on the shoulder of the road.

The attacker's horse laid still, its head twisted at an odd

angle. *Apparently broke its neck in the fall,* Flood thought.

McGinnis stumbled through the brush to his side, blue eyes wide. "By the . . . by the. . . ."

"By the balls of Beelzebub!" Flood furnished the flustered professor.

McGinnis shot him a sharp glance. "Are you mocking me?"

"No. That's just the way I feel," Flood said, a long breath whistling through his teeth. "That's twice in two days." With shaking hands he absently began punching the empty shells out of his pistol. "It's time we start traveling by dark." He hadn't the faintest idea what they would do now, but dusk was coming on.

Flood scrambled up onto the road. McGinnis followed, clutching the small leather pouch with its precious papers. The professor stooped to examine the cylindrical helmet while Flood confirmed the horse was dead. The saddle was not antique, but rather the standard Western type.

"Get back into those trees and wait for me," Flood said. "There may be more of them. Our horse shouldn't have gone far. I'm going to see if I can catch up with him before it gets dark. Give me twenty or thirty minutes."

"Then what?"

"I'll be back with or without him. But I don't relish walking the rest of the way to Nashville."

McGinnis nodded and headed promptly for the cover of the thick timber. Flood finished reloading his Colt, snapped the loading gate shut, and jogged away down the road.

He was back as dusk was fading into night, leading the unharnessed gray by the long reins he had looped over his arm. "McGinnis!" he called softly.

"Here."

Flood saw the shadowy figure coming out of hiding, lugging the saddle and bridle from the dead horse. They saddled the gray.

"There's a farm back up the road about a mile. The barn's near the road. Let's see if we can slip in there and sleep a few hours. We'll head out before dawn."

The adrenaline had ebbed, and Flood now felt drained, exhausted. Yet he made the older man mount up while he himself led the horse. They found the deserted barn silhouetted against the moonlit sky and slipped inside. Flood struck a match, located and lighted a lantern hanging on a post. "No worry about the farmer seeing the light," he said. "The house is a good quarter mile back up yonder in those trees. Just keep the lantern low and behind the wall."

They forked down some hay into one of the stalls for the horse and sat down in the next stall in the dusty straw, the smoky lantern on the bare ground between them.

"We're safe enough here for the night. I don't think this barn has been used lately, except for storing hay," Flood said, his voice dull with fatigue.

The two men sat silently for several minutes.

Finally Flood said: "It's about time you gave me an explanation. I think I've earned it." He looked steadily at the lean professor who was cradling the metal helmet he'd retrieved from the road. McGinnis did not meet his gaze for several long seconds. Twigs and leaves were stuck to his wool jacket, and there was a scratch on his forehead. His thick, white hair was in wild disarray. McGinnis raked his fingers through his hair and said: "I'm paying you well for your protection. You'd be better off not knowing."

"I want to know, Mac. Any secrets you may have are safe with me. I'm certainly not going to make any judgments about anyone being in trouble with the law."

"Hell, did those men look like the law to you?" he snorted.

Then he took a deep breath and set the helmet aside. "Well, you asked for it," he began. "Have you ever heard of the Knights Templar?"

"As a matter of fact I saw a reference to them about a month ago. Researching the history of the Cistercian order in the monastery library. Bunch of knights in the Middle Ages."

"Huh! Bunch of knights? That's like calling a tornado a dust devil. They were the most powerful and richest order of knights in the entire medieval world!" McGinnis paused, as if not quite sure how to proceed. "Let me simplify all this for you. The Knights of the Temple were formed in Jerusalem during the First Crusade for the purpose of fighting the infidels and protecting travelers to the Holy Land. Over the next two hundred years they grew in wealth and power exceeding the Teutonic Knights and the Hospitalers, their closest rivals. These orders often fought each other, but that's another story. The Templars were falsely accused of heresy, homosexuality, and worshipping of idols. They were disbanded abruptly in Thirteen-Oh-Seven by the King of France and the Pope. Templar property and wealth were confiscated by the king, who was in financial trouble. Gold and silver of all kinds had been stashed in the Knights' temple in Paris when the Grand Master was recalled from Cyprus by King Philip the Fair. A group of Templars, who escaped arrest, managed to sneak the treasure out of the temple and later took it to Scotland. Even though the order was officially disbanded, many of the knights kept the Templars functioning as an underground order. In the early Fifteen Hundreds, the treasure in Scotland was in danger of being discovered, and a small group of knights sailed with the treasure to the New World where it was hidden. All but one of this small group died of disease or starvation or at the hands of Indians. Peter Stirling, the lone survivor, returned to Scotland but perished of fever in prison without revealing the location of the treasure." He paused and looked directly at Flood. "After years of persistent research . . . and a little luck . . . I've discovered the diary Peter Stirling kept on this journey."

"So you know where this treasure is, and someone is trying to prevent you from getting to it?" Flood finished, hoping the skepticism didn't creep into his tone.

McGinnis nodded, his usual snappish manner subdued.

"Who?" Flood asked.

"Modern Templars. Or, I should say, a splinter group of the modern Templars."

"Splinter group?"

"Aye, laddy. Even the Church itself hasn't been free of schism. And this group that began as warrior monks hasn't either. As near as I can estimate, this splinter group numbers no more than two or three hundred. But they are much more violent and ambitious than the larger body of Templars. Their aim is to reëstablish a new version of the Holy Roman Empire."

"You're joking! Like the one Charlemagne declared in the year Eight Hundred supposedly to replace the old Roman Empire?"

"Correct . . . only on a modern scale. One government for all of Europe ruled by these talented and vicious men, just as the Emperors and the Roman Senate ruled the ancient world. You can see that a fabulous wealth of treasure would go far toward financing their aims, raising armies, bribing heads of state, and so forth."

"What's all the medieval get-up for? If they're serious about killing you, why use lances and crossbows?"

"Both deadly weapons. . . ."

"I'm sure in the early Middle Ages they were the latest arms, but why now?"

"Fear is also a great weapon, laddy."

"Maybe for some fool who knows nothing about this organization. But why try to scare *you?*"

"If I'm found skewered with a lance and someone reports seeing knights in armor, it will certainly frighten anyone else from trying to find their treasure. Word will be put out and the superstition spread that some six-hundred-year-old knights are still protecting the Templar treasure . . . provided I spread the word that the treasure really exists. That's part of what my lecture will be about at the ISHA conference." He indicated the pouch beside him. "I'm risking my reputation on this presentation. I'll either be laughed out of my position at the university, or I'll be famous. Not only will I be written up in professional journals, but I'll be in the newspapers . . . a celebrity, lecturing all over the country." He spread his hands, blue eyes snapping in the lantern light. "Kids will read about me in their history books a hundred years from now."

"But these modern Templars are not taking any chances?" Flood asked to bring him back on track.

McGinnis nodded dumbly, patting the pouch beside him. "You or anyone else could read my notes, but they'd make no sense at all since they're written in a code, a sort of shorthand of my own devising. And this is the only copy. Of course, my notes are based on Stirling's journal. Besides the archaic wording, I doubt you could read his atrocious handwriting, anyway. Apparently it was written on the march in all kinds of weather. Some of it is indecipherable, even to me."

"So they want your notes and you dead." Flood paused, then added: "You have this journal with you?"

"What kind of a fool do you take me for? It's in a safe place in Chicago. Somehow they know I've found the diary."

"The Templars can't find the treasure without that book . . . or your notes, which they can't read?" Flood said.

"Never underestimate the enemy. I'm sure someone in their order is smart enough to break my rather simple code."

Flood thought that making this eccentric old man look ridiculous in the public eye would probably be a more effective policy. *Reductio ad absurdum*—a debating technique to discredit one's opponent. If nobody took such a wild assertion seriously, that would be the end of the McGinnis threat. The only way he could be vindicated would be actually to produce the treasure. Flood had a sudden twinge of doubt. Maybe he was the one who was a fool for believing this strange-acting old man he really knew nothing about.

"This is no civic organization," McGinnis continued, with some sarcasm in his voice. "It is a secret society of bloodshed, terror, bribery, and extortion! They've moved a long way from their original purpose."

"I take it they've shed their image as a monastic order, too?" Flood remarked dryly.

McGinnis nodded. "They were the bankers for governments. They owned castles everywhere. They had tax-free status. Collections were taken up for them in churches. They were answerable only to the Pope in spiritual matters." His voice became low and urgent. "You can't imagine what a power the Templars were . . . much greater than the Hospitalers or the Teutonic Knights, the other two major fighting orders of the day. In fact, their power was the main reason for their downfall. King Philip the Fair of France was in debt to them . . . and he feared their political power and their potential force of arms. That's why he pressured Pope Clement the Fifth, a Frenchman, into bringing them to trial for heresy and abolishing the order. They were tortured by the Inquisitors to force confessions of heresy and homosexuality and worshipping of idols. The last Grand Master of the Templars, Jacques de Molay, was burned at the stake in Thirteen Fourteen. The curse he called down on the heads of King Philip the Fair and the Pope apparently worked." McGinnis almost smiled. "The Pope died within thirty days, and the king died within a year of de Molay's execution."

"I thought the only thing left of that order were a few of their ceremonies later adopted by the Masonic lodge."

"Not by the hammer of Saint Joseph! Their successors are here, hundreds of years later, and stronger than ever. This splinter group has been denounced by the majority of the modern Templar order, but a couple hundred of the rebels occupy positions of influence, several dozen of them in this country. Members of a secret society . . . a brotherhood of wealthy knights . . . influential politicians, bankers, businessmen, publishers . . . all of them ruthlessly seeking power and riches with the ultimate goal of reëstablishing the Holy Roman Empire."

"Ridiculous!"

"I'm sure that's what they'd like you to believe. But, remember, several of the crowned heads of Europe are currently related by blood. A few strong alliances, many millions of dollars in gold to finance some private bribes, and a well-placed and dedicated army. . . ." He shrugged. "It's happened before. Who's to say it couldn't happen again?"

Flood shook his head in disbelief.

"That's why I'm saying that exposure to the gaze of the world would be like strong sunlight to a fungus," McGinnis went on. "If it didn't kill them, the damage would radically reduce their power for years to come."

"Seems like they'd run the risk of being discovered if they liquidate an ancient treasure to fill their coffers."

"Without undue notice, it could be sold off piecemeal to museums and collectors around the world. They would likely keep the most precious artifacts as their one rallying point and physical link with the past. The Templar leaders would as soon sell these as Queen Victoria would sell the crown jewels of England." McGinnis had risen to his feet and was now pacing in the stall, waving his arms, his lean face suffused with color. "At the current market value of gold and silver, this treasure is undoubtedly worth millions. As ancient works of art and rare coins, it is worth even more to collectors and museums."

"Not the bank account from your average fraternity dues."

The professor nodded. "Except for lip service, they've completely abandoned the spiritual side of the order." He paused and smiled. "But I think you put the fear of God into a couple of them. When your bullet grooved the side of that helmet, I can imagine what it must have sounded like."

"Like putting your head in a metal trash can and hitting the side of it with a club," Flood said. "And I also shot him in the shoulder or upper arm."

"Chain mail is no defense against a modern missile, just as it was no defense against the hacking of a broadsword or a well-aimed crossbow," the professor said. "By the way, did you know that Richard the First, the Lion Heart, was killed by a crossbow?"

"No, I didn't."

The professor seemed to ooze irrelevant information and obscure facts. One of the hazards of his profession, Flood guessed, staring off into the dark corners of the barn where shadows from the lantern danced and wavered. He hardly dared believe this tale, but he really had no reason not to. After all, there was the proof of two attacks in two days by mounted men wearing armor and carrying weapons straight out of the 12th Century. One of the horsemen wore the red cross on a white mantle—granted as their official symbol by an early pope. Flood thought the name Knights Templar didn't even sound Christian, but it was derived from the order having been founded in a captured Jerusalem mosque built on the site of Solomon's temple.

"Greek fire," McGinnis said.

"What?" Flood tried to focus.

"That's probably what was on those crossbow arrows to cause such an instant flash fire. And from the white glare, I'd guess there was some magnesium in it as well."

"What's Greek fire?" Flood vaguely remembered hearing the term before, possibly in connection to the War Between the States.

"It's a chemical mixture that ignites and burns furiously when it comes in contact with water. The arrows were probably wrapped with tubes of water and the chemical separately so they'd burst and splatter on contact. The Byzantine Greeks first used it in a naval battle in Six Seventy-Three. Nobody knows for sure of what it was made, but probably had sulphur, resin, oil, pitch, and maybe quicklime. Later, naphtha, saltpeter, and turpentine were added. It acts a lot like liquid gunpowder."

"So they even used an ancient method of burning up our buggy," Flood marveled. "The early Templars recaptured Jerusalem in the First Crusade. Apparently they were a lot more efficient than this bunch."

"From all accounts, the early Templars fought with a ferocity that struck terror into the Moslems. But the majority of the members, many of whom weren't knights, were better at building castles, acquiring money, and administering large holdings than fighting," the professor said.

"The warrior monks . . . ," Flood mused. "What an anomaly! Saint Bernard of Clairvaux wrote a justification of their fighting for Christ. I read a translation of it in the

Gethsemani library. The first Christian justification of holy war."

"Ah, yes, Bernard, abbot of the monastery at Clairvaux," the professor mused. "A founder of the Cistercian order of monks, later known as the Trappists."

Flood nodded. "I was researching the history of the order and discovered him."

"He also drafted the written Rule for the Templars, along the same lines as that of the Cistercians."

"I didn't know that." The thought of Saint Bernard brought the old familiar stab of doubt to his innards. The apparent conflict of this teaching on war had tortured him off and on for months. But now was not the time to drag all that up again. With a conscious effort, he set the thought aside to concentrate on the problems at hand.

He was hungry, thirsty, tired, and dirty, as was the man he was supposed to be guarding. "Get some rest," he heard himself saying to McGinnis. "We'll be up and out of here before daylight."

McGinnis laid the helmet aside and stretched out on the straw, propping himself up on an elbow. "There's one other thing about the Templars you should probably know," he said. "In the Fifteenth Century they built an exact replica of the Temple of Solomon in Rosslyn, Scotland. The building is now known as the Rosslyn Chapel. Legend has it that the Israelites constructed four or five Arks of the Covenant to hold the stone tablets on which God had inscribed the original Ten Commandments. Why the Jews would do this, I have no idea, and there's no written documentation of it that I can find. Anyway, the early Templars supposedly dug up one of these Arks from under the site of the Temple of Solomon in Jerusalem around the year Eleven Hundred and much later brought it to Rosslyn, Scotland, which to this day remains at least the nominal spiritual center of the Templars." He gave a snort of disbelief. "You can take that for what it's worth, because I don't know of a single living soul who's laid eyes on that Ark. Allegedly it's buried deep under the Rosslyn Chapel. I only tell you this because I think the Rosslyn Chapel story is just a smoke screen . . . a diversion, if you will, to distract scholars from the real treasure hidden in the American West."

And I'm a member of the Flat Earth Society, Flood thought. All this talk of treasure and secret societies he'd found fascinating at first, but now it'd taken on the aspect of a ghost story told around the campfire at a children's summer camp. His eyelids were growing heavy from boredom, disbelief, or just plain fatigue—he didn't know which. But he had to get some sleep. "I don't think there's any need to keep watch," he said. "I'm certain no one saw us come in here." He leaned over and turned the lantern down until the flame was snuffed. Ghostly moonlight shone through a gap in the dilapidated roof. He stretched out with a groan of aching muscles. "The cold will wake me before dawn," he said by way of a good night.

Chapter Four

Vanderbilt University
Nashville, Tennessee

Merliss McGinnis spent a miserable night. She chose to sleep in her clothes, pulling the quilt up after removing only her high-top shoes. Even though she felt smothered by the tight bodice and voluminous petticoats and skirt, she wanted to be ready for any chance at escape. Anderson, her captor and guard, never left the dormitory room on the Vanderbilt campus. He sat on the floor with his back to the door, a pillow propped behind his head, and dozed. Merliss had been mortified by having to use the slop jar in the presence of this man, although, she had to admit, Anderson at least looked away and pretended disinterest.

Several times she had awakened during the night, her arms tensely clutching the quilt to her chin. She wasn't troubled by fearful dreams, but she certainly didn't rest.

The ham sandwiches and coffee, that another man had brought about mid-afternoon, still sat on her stomach like a lead weight when she awoke the last time to see gray light filtering in under the half-drawn shade of the single window.

Anderson lay slumped against the door, mouth ajar, suit rumpled, and the butt of a pistol showing from a shoulder holster.

By noon today she should be freed from this kidnapping, and she could go to the police. Or could she? If Anderson kept his word and released her, it would be at the cost of her uncle's freedom, or his life. Anderson had not said what he and his friends, whoever they were, planned to do with Uncle Mac. And if they didn't get him, she would still be held prisoner. She had no idea what this was all about. She had somehow to get away, to intercept her uncle who would probably be arriving sometime before noon today.

But how? She was helpless against this man. What weapons did she have?—guile and feminine charm, rather than force. They would be dangerous and might very well backfire on her. But she had to try. She'd grown up in Chicago and had dealt with young men before, but some of them were just crude and obvious, rather than actually dangerous. As the room grew lighter with the coming dawn, she steeled herself for the effort.

The earliest rays of sunlight were slanting obliquely through the dusty windowpane when Anderson gaped and stretched. He struggled to his feet, rubbing his eyes and rotating his head.

"Damn! Got a crick in my neck," he growled. He looked at her, then pulled out a watch from a vest pocket. "Our breakfast should be here in about an hour." He managed a tight smile. "And before lunch time, you and I will part company. I'm sure you'll be glad to see the last of me."

"Well, actually, I've grown quite used to you," she replied, giving him a sidelong glance.

"Well, it's good that you aren't afraid of me, because I have no intention of harming you, lady."

"I can sense that. And you can call me Merliss." She smiled. "I wish there was something to do to pass the time. I've read that newspaper from front to back." She ran her fingers through her dark hair. "I need to freshen up. Any chance I could go down the hall to see if there's an indoor bathroom in this building?"

He shook his head. "Sorry."

"Can't even brush my teeth. You don't happen to have a nip of something on you that would change the taste in my mouth?"

She saw his eyes take on a mischievous gleam. "I just might." He produced a thin flask from an inside coat pocket. "Apricot brandy."

"My very favorite," she smiled, swallowing her revulsion.

Anderson uncapped it, took a swig, swirled it around in his mouth, and swallowed. He held it out to her.

Merliss took the flask, held her breath, and took a gulp, trying not to taste it. The sweet liquid burnt all the way down. "Marvelous," she breathed.

"Have another."

"Maybe later," she replied, dangling her legs over the side of the bed. "Meanwhile, why don't you sit down here and tell me something about yourself. I'm sure a man as rugged and handsome as yourself has had some interesting adventures."

She could see him swell with confidence as he turned the key in the door lock and joined her on the bed.

"Well, now, Merliss, I just may have a few stories you'd get a thrill out of hearing. . . ."

A half hour later, she was in her chemise and Anderson's suit lay crumpled on the floor, along with his shoulder harness and gun. She willed herself to be somewhere else as she kissed him, feeling the stubble of his beard and smelling the bay rum. She was using all her wiles, seeming to give in, little by little, yet stalling, teasing, maneuvering.

"Is that a cut on your neck?" he murmured, nuzzling her.

"No." She could feel her face flaming. "It's a birthmark." The three-inch long red blemish on her neck embarrassed her even more than being half undressed. The mark was shaped roughly like the island of England and Scotland, and she'd

49

taken pains for years to keep it covered.

"Oh, Robert, I'm getting so warm. Let me open that window. . . ."

"Just slip out of those duds, honey. That'll help."

"No . . . no, I need some air. But I'll bet you can be out of those drawers before I get back from the window. Is it a bet?" she teased.

"You got it," he panted, grunting as he pulled off the remainder of his underwear.

She slid off the bed, surreptitiously shoving his clothes and the gun underneath as she shuffled toward the window.

She twisted open the lock on the window, distracting him with a wicked smile. He was stark naked on the bed. She yanked the window all the way up. With one quick, backward glance, she vaulted through the opening and sprinted away, barefoot, through the cold, dew-drenched grass.

Clad only in bloomers and camisole, and spurred by the adrenaline of fear, her feet flew over the ground to the end of the building. Just as she turned the corner of the brick dormitory, she heard Anderson bellowing a curse behind her. He wouldn't dare follow without clothes, so she knew she had a decent head start.

"Help!" she screamed. "Help! A man is after me!" But the few students walking across campus merely stared at her curiously as she ran in panic. Where was the administration building? Would anybody be in the president's office this early? Probably not. But conference attendees were already filtering toward the meeting hall in the Vanderbilt gymnasium on West End Avenue. She remembered from the printed schedule that coffee and pastries were being served to everyone starting at seven that morning.

Gasping, she burst through the double doors into the hall and staggered against two well-dressed men conversing by a table loaded with food. A coffee cup went clattering.

"By God, what's this?" one of the men cried, grasping her before she could fall.

"Help! Please help me. Man trying to kill me! Call police!" Her breath came in ragged gasps. "Rape!" she added for good measure. In her half-dressed state, she knew this one word would bring the right reaction. No sense trying to explain anything as complicated as her abduction.

"Settle down, now," the second man said as three or four more quickly gathered around her. "No one's going to hurt you."

"He's got a gun!" she gasped.

"Don't worry, miss. You're safe with us. Who is this man?"

"Calls himself Robert Anderson. Big man . . . with black mustache. Held me captive . . . all night in a dormitory room . . . over there somewhere." She pointed in the general direction.

Several women had also gathered, and someone produced a linen tablecloth, wrapping it around her shoulders. Only then did Merliss realize that she was shaking.

"What's your name?" one of the men asked.

"Don't be questioning her now, George," a buxom, older woman admonished. "Can't you see the poor child needs to get some clothes? Here, dear." The woman thrust a cup of hot coffee into her hands. Merliss sipped it gratefully.

"My name is Merliss McGinnis," she replied, her breathing beginning to steady down. "I was to meet my uncle, Professor Roddy McGinnis. He's scheduled to lecture here today."

"Oh, yes," a stocky, bearded man said with enthusiasm. "McGinnis's niece. I'm looking forward to hearing what Roddy has to say. Haven't seen him in three years. Rumor has it he's going to throw a bombshell into the middle of this stuffy conference. Knowing him, it could be 'most anything.'"

As the minutes dragged on, Merliss eyed the door, but Anderson did not appear, and her panic began to subside. But another fear crept into her consciousness. Anderson indicated he was not in this alone. Others were at this conference who were going to intercept her uncle. And at least one man, whose face she had not seen, had brought them food while she was confined. She'd better not say much, since enemies might be within earshot. From remarks she was hearing around her, her uncle had not yet made an appearance. If he were true to his usual habit, he would walk in at the last minute, looking disheveled, pull out a handful of notes, and begin lecturing. He was not one to arrive early and socialize with his peers.

"We'll send someone for your clothes. Where were you?"

She hesitated. "I can't describe it. I'll have to show you. The man has a gun."

"Don't worry. Several of us will go. He won't try anything," replied the lean, muscular man who'd first caught her.

She picked a cinnamon roll from the table as they escorted her, still wrapped in the tablecloth, toward the door.

As she suspected, the room where she'd spent the last twenty-four hours, was empty, except for her clothing, which she retrieved and put on.

"We can call the police, miss, but without more to go on, I'm afraid they won't be able to do much," the stocky, bearded man said, "and I'm very much afraid your attacker is long gone."

"He is, if he knows what's good for him," another man added.

"Where's the road coming into Nashville from Kentucky?" she asked, knowing that she had to try to catch her uncle before he got here.

"There's more than one. Are you leaving? Are you sure you're all right?"

"I'm fine now," Merliss replied, forcing a smile. "But I have to reach my uncle."

"Isn't he going to come here?"

"I must reach him before he arrives," she said, trying to evade any further questions as she sidled away.

The man explained how to reach both of the main roads from the north by going back through downtown.

"I'll catch the streetcar," she said, starting away and wondering what would happen if she failed to intercept him.

"Maybe I should hail a cab for you," the lean man said, catching up with her as she emerged from the dormitory. She knew the man was concerned for her safety but not quite sure how far to push himself on her. Her youthful good looks had never failed to elicit help from strange men, but now she just wanted to be alone, without answering any more questions. "Just walk me to the street and wait with me until the trolley comes," she said.

Ten minutes later she was aboard the clanging, clattering inbound streetcar full of men on their way to work in the downtown area. The coffee and pastry had renewed her energy, and, in spite of her restless sleep and frantic flight, she was feeling reasonably good. But finding her uncle was going to be a very chancy thing. If she couldn't locate him before noon, she'd have to assume he'd gotten past her and have to return to the campus to look for him. If she could somehow find Uncle Mac in time, surely he'd have some idea what they were dealing with. Even in the crowded trolley, she found herself looking at the other passengers, wondering if one or more of the men sitting around her might be part of this conspiracy, whatever it was—some potential enemy who was ready to snatch her as she stepped off the car. She knew she was becoming paranoid, seeing hostile eyes everywhere.

As the trolley clattered and jerked around a curve into another street toward the state capitol, she again turned her gaze out the window beside her. They were passing the smoky, brick railroad dépôt. Passengers milled about on the platform.

Suddenly a flash of white hair caught her eye among the many men wearing hats. She focused on the moving figure, and her heart leaped. It was Uncle Mac! She sprang out of her seat. "Stop! Stop! Let me off!" She yanked the bell cord and quickly moved to the front door.

"Next corner, lady."

"No. Stop here. I want out!"

With a look of resignation, the operator drew the car to a halt, and Merliss bounced out into the street, narrowly missing a passing delivery wagon.

By the time she got to the wooden platform of the old dépôt, she didn't see the white head. "Uncle Mac! Roddy McGinnis!" she cried frantically, pushing through the thinning group of passengers, looking here and there, trying to see between the heads and shoulders, ignoring the looks and comments.

"Merliss? Is that you?"

"Uncle Mac!"

The uncle she knew so well was suddenly hugging her. She buried her face in his shoulder, muttering: "Thank God. Thank God I found you!"

"It's great to see you. But you didn't have to come here to meet me. Say, how did you know I was coming by train instead of buggy?" He held her at arm's length, and she felt tears of relief running down her cheeks.

"Why, is something the matter?"

She tried to swallow the lump in her throat. "Uncle Mac, let's get out of this crowd. I have to talk to you."

"Merliss, I'd like you to meet someone. This is Marcus Flood. He's my bodyguard . . . and fresh out of the monastery."

"How do you do?" she muttered distractedly.

"Let's go into the dépôt restaurant. I'm hungry," McGinnis said.

The three found a table out of earshot of other patrons, and Merliss gave a quick summary of her abduction.

He uncle's face clouded. "I was afraid something like this would happen."

"What's going on, Uncle Mac?" she cried, trying to keep her voice steady.

McGinnis glanced around and lowered his voice. "By the sword of Damocles," he grated, "I regret putting you in danger. But I might have known they'd do almost anything to get their hands on me and my notes before I made my presentation to the ISHA." He briefly related the tale of the diary that would point the way to the Templar treasure. As he spoke, she found her stomach tightening with fear and wonder at the danger.

"It all makes sense now," she said slowly, when he finally paused. "But it's a lot worse than I imagined. At least, you're not part of some criminal activity."

She looked at this Marc Flood, an extraordinarily handsome man, and tried to reconcile his being a bodyguard *and* a former monk. Apparently he was very good as a guard from the exploits her uncle had just described. She gave him a closer inspection, without appearing obvious about it—dark brown, wavy hair, a rakish smile, with haunting hazel eyes. His athletic build and work-coarsened hands, along with the brown stubble on his lean, tanned cheeks, belied any sedentary occupation.

"So," McGinnis continued, "about four this morning we rode away from that barn to town just in time to sell the horse to the station master and catch the Dixie Flyer. I sure hated to lose that gray. Best harness horse I ever had."

"If these men are out to intercept you, they're probably watching the railroad station," Flood remarked.

It was the first time he'd contributed anything to the conversation, and Merliss looked at him as he shifted in his chair to scan the crowd. She noticed that he carried a revolver in a shoulder holster under his jacket. In spite of the danger they were in, she found herself wanting to know this man better.

"Are you still determined to give that speech?" Flood asked.

McGinnis said nothing.

"Oh, please don't, Uncle Mac," Merliss said, a memory of the terror she'd endured at the hands of Robert Anderson flashing through her mind. "Those Templars, or whoever they are, are out to kill you. I know they're waiting for you at the campus. Let's get away from here . . . now!"

The professor was silent for a long minute. The he muttered: "I hate to let those jackals run me off."

"Do you think anyone will believe you really found Peter Stirling's diary, since you didn't bring it with you?" Flood asked.

"I'll submit it to the proper experts for verification when the time comes," he said. "This is just the first announcement."

"Wouldn't it be better to locate the treasure first and then make your announcement?" Merliss asked.

"That's right," Flood agreed. "Then there'd be no doubt. With no preliminary public announcement, you'd deal the

Templars a heavy blow and make yourself rich at the same time."

"By the veil of Veronica, you may be right!" the older man exclaimed, his face lighting up. "These assassins have pushed me far enough! Before I publicize my find, the two of you will come with me on the hunt. By the head of John the Baptist, we'll find that treasure first! Once the three of us have split that huge stash of ancient gold, then let my critics call me crazy!"

Merliss had always made allowances for her uncle's odd ideas and behavior. Now she took a deep breath, knowing the time had come to excuse herself. There was no way she wanted to be involved in such a wild, dangerous, and probably futile expedition. But she knew from experience that Uncle Mac was obstinate as well as somewhat addled. Now that he'd made up his mind, it might be impossible for her to squirm away.

Chapter Five

En Route

Marc Flood sat on a green velvet window seat in the day coach and watched a man running to swing aboard the train as it rolled slowly out of the Nashville station. Flood considered it odd that the man had no luggage. But it was possible he had already been a passenger and had just gotten off for a time at the Nashville stop and was late reboarding. But Flood could take no chances. He memorized the look of this individual—over six feet tall, about his own age, broad shoulders, and big hands, hair somewhat longer than fashionable, and clean-shaven. He wore a dark suit with a collarless white shirt.

Flood had seen this man observing the three of them as they sat in the dépôt restaurant. Probably imagining enemies where there are none, Flood thought. Just the kind of fear the real Templars hoped to inspire.

As the late boarder came through his coach, Flood slouched in his seat with a newspaper over his face as if asleep until the man departed into the next car forward. Flood couldn't believe he'd let Roddy McGinnis talk him into continuing as his bodyguard. But the two attacks they'd already endured convinced him the threat to the professor was real. And the story Merliss McGinnis related sealed his belief in some terrible plot afoot to capture and kill the aged scholar. Flood was not yet sure if he believed the story about the

Templar treasure, but some group was certainly taking the old man seriously about something.

He sighed and looked out the window. On a sunny hill in the near distance the American flag snapped in the breeze above the massive state capitol building. The jumbled structures of Nashville began to slide past them as the train picked up speed and swung into a long left-hand curve toward Memphis, more than two hundred miles to the southwest. There was no use lying to himself. The one convincing argument in favor of his taking this train was the presence of a very frightened Merliss McGinnis. More to the point were her incredible blue eyes. Flood had never seen anything like those pale, aquamarine pools. Soft eyes they were, and kind, yet with intelligence behind them. And, even though he'd listened carefully to her tale of daring and decisive escape, the eyes looked somehow vulnerable. He could well understand how her captor had been mesmerized long enough to be fooled.

Roddy McGinnis and his niece were riding in the next car ahead of him as the train pulled away. By the time McGinnis had convinced the two of them to venture West by rail with him to find the treasure, they'd had no time to buy tickets. They'd just boarded and taken seats in separate cars a minute or so before the locomotive began chuffing its way out of the station.

"We can buy our tickets when the conductor comes around," McGinnis had said. None of them had any luggage—not so much as a toothbrush among them. Merliss had wanted at least to secure her bag and extra clothing from her boarding house, but her uncle would not delay that long. He told her she could deal with that later, that their lives were more important.

All this was running through Flood's mind as he got up and leisurely followed the man he'd been watching. He passed between the cars and paused just inside the door of the next coach. His gaze swept the passengers. The car was about half full. McGinnis and his niece sat on opposite sides, conversing across the aisle. Flood saw the late arrival sitting several seats behind them. Flood slid into the nearest empty seat to keep an eye on the situation.

They'd not had time to eat anything at the dépôt restaurant, and Flood's stomach was rumbling. He guessed from the sun it was about noon. There was a dining car on this train, and maybe the train would also make a stop or two along the way. If so, they might get off and take the next train, just to confuse anyone who might be tailing them, such as the man who was sitting nearby—a man who could just be waiting a chance at the professor. Flood would have to make sure that chance never came. He was beginning to feel like a lean and hungry wolf protecting a litter of pups. He had never done this kind of work in his checkered career, but his military experience and discipline came back to him. He felt he had an instinct for survival.

An hour later, when the conductor arrived, McGinnis paid for all three tickets. The thin, uniformed man was not happy about this irregularity, but took the money, punched the cardboard tickets, and handed them over. As he passed on down the aisle, he replied to Flood's question that they had, indeed, boarded an express that was to make no stops, other than for water, during the Memphis run.

They waited until shortly before the dining car stopped serving before going forward to get something to eat. Flood's suspicions were strengthened when the late boarder followed them into the dining car. Speaking *sotto voce,* Flood told them about the man he suspected was following them. This news didn't appear to faze McGinnis. But Merliss seemed tense and had trouble eating the steak and potatoes she'd ordered.

"Don't worry," Flood said. "I can't be certain he's one of the Templars. But if he doesn't make a move before we get to Memphis tonight, we'll give him the slip and take another train to Saint Louis."

"What?" McGinnis arched his brows. "By the rock of Saint Peter, that's not the way we want to go!"

"I know," Flood continued in a soothing voice. "If this man thinks that the treasure is hidden in the Southwest, he'd never expect us to head north. We're just taking a detour." He felt much more in command now, much more energized since eating a good meal.

"Humph!" McGinnis clearly didn't like Flood's idea, but seemed to be considering it.

"If you want me to protect you, let me make the decisions," Flood urged, glancing at Merliss for support. All he got was distracted by those eyes.

"We'll see," McGinnis said, apparently not wanting to commit himself ahead of time.

And that's where the matter lay for the rest of the afternoon as Flood roamed restlessly up and down the train, never straying far from the two McGinnises. When he allowed himself a few minutes to look, he observed the greening hills and farms of west Tennessee unfolding past the windows. At several of the water stops, he stood on the platform between the cars to breathe the fresh April air and felt himself beginning to regain the sense of calm that had been disrupted by events of the last three days. It was the never-changing, yet ever-changing cycles and rhythms of the seasons he had come to know intimately as a lay brother, working in the fields. He saw the hand of the Creator in the greening of spring, but felt estranged from it now that he had chosen to come back to the violence of the world and human conflict. But he had to admit that the inner conflict that had driven him out of the

61

monastery was nearly as wrenching.

As dusk came on, the locomotive was thundering through the thick, forested flatlands some thirty miles east of the bluff city of Memphis. Flood's thin layer of tranquility was shattered when he encountered McGinnis in the aisle of the coach. "Where are you going? To the toilet?"

"Stand aside, man. By the foamy flagon of Falstaff, I need a drink! The bar car is that way."

"Uncle Mac, don't go. We'll be in Memphis soon," Merliss pleaded, catching up and hooking her arm through his elbow.

Flood shot her a sharp glance, wondering what was behind her concern.

"Saint Elmo's fire!" he exploded. "I've never let a woman tell me what to do, and I don't plan to start now." He pulled away from her and elbowed past Flood, leaving several of the nearby passengers staring after him.

"What's up?" Flood queried her quietly.

"He's the best relative anyone could have," she replied sadly, "except when he's drinking. He just gets crazy after only a couple of shots. He can't tolerate alcohol."

"This sure isn't the time to start boozing," Flood agreed.

"Go after him, Marc," she begged. "You can persuade him to come back. He trusts you."

Flood was glad he couldn't see those limpid eyes in the gradually darkening coach. He silently gritted his teeth in frustration. Things were dangerous enough without taking on the added responsibility of protecting the eccentric professor from himself as well. He took a deep breath and blew out his cheeks.

"Please," she said softly.

He crumbled like sand before an ocean wave. "All right," he replied, touching her shoulder reassuringly, as he started toward the end door where McGinnis had disappeared.

As he stepped out into the windy darkness and closed the door behind him, he heard a strangled yelp of terror only a few feet away, and the professor fell backward into him. Flood brushed him aside and swung around to face another shadowy figure lunging out of the shadows. He caught the man with a short, hard uppercut in the mid-section. The muscle sheath gave only a little, but he heard the air *whoosh* out as the attacker was staggered. McGinnis was struggling to get out of the way as the man came for him again. But the jerking and swaying of the train threw off his balance, and the upward arc of the knife clanged off the unseen iron hand rail, flipping the knife out of the attacker's hand. It skittered away across the metal platform.

Like a hunting panther, Flood landed on the man's back before he could straighten. With a roar, the man reared up and flung Flood off like he was a pesky house cat, slamming him back against the door. Stunned by the impact, Flood slid to a sitting position. His dazed mind finally commanded his hand to reach for his gun. But his reaction was too slow, and a fist slammed into the side of his head, knocking him to his hands and knees. A hand grabbed the back of his collar and another the tail of his jacket, skidding him toward the edge of the platform. With a desperate lunge, he twisted onto his back, breaking the hold. He clutched frantically upward, and his hands closed on coat lapels. With one continuous motion, he thrust up with both feet into the groin, flipping the bigger man heels over head into the darkness. It was over so quickly, he hardly realized his instincts had saved him as he lay, gasping, on his back, his head hanging off the edge of the swaying platform. Then he got hold of the hand rail and pulled himself back aboard. He struggled to his knees and looked off into the thick woods that were flashing past. The train rumbled over a small, wooden bridge, and he smelled the dank water of the swampy lowland.

His breath came in raspy gasps, and he turned to find McGinnis.

"By the powers of Heaven, did you get that damned Templar?" the professor's shaky voice came from the darkness. The old man stood up from where he'd been crouching on the platform of the adjoining car.

"How do you know he was a Templar?" Flood gasped.

"Hell's heat, man! Who else would be after me?"

"Right you are," Flood panted. The odds of a chance robber attacking the old man were long, at best. He put a hand to the side of his head where a fist had caught him. He'd have a lump there for sure. He wondered if the man he'd flung off, maybe to his death, was the one he'd been watching. Even though Flood fancied himself to be in good physical condition, the unseen assailant seemed much stronger. For a few seconds he visualized a hundred men like that—tall and hard-muscled, clad in chain mail and astride big horses as they rode across arid deserts of the Near East toward Jerusalem. It took little imagination to picture himself up against a formidable foe of the 11th Century.

Then he shook himself like a wet dog and forced the thought from his mind. "Are you hurt?" he asked. "Did he get you with that knife?"

"Scuffed a bit, laddy, but none the worse for it, no thanks to you."

Resentment welled up in Flood at this callous ingratitude. "He got in the first thrust, maybe," he spat, "but you'd be leaking like a sieve right now if I hadn't come after you as quick as I did. If you'd stayed within my sight instead of going off after a drink, this wouldn't have happened." He shook his head. "Well, no matter. He'd have found some other place to attack you, if not here and now."

The rattling and banging of the coupling and the clatter and screeching of the wheels and undercarriage had apparently kept the struggle from being heard inside either coach, since no one had appeared to investigate. This was probably why the attacker had used a knife instead of a gun. The knife! He shoved McGinnis aside and crouched on the platform to look for the weapon he'd seen fly out of the man's hand. The light from the window in the door revealed the dull gleam of a blade. He retrieved the attacker's knife, and the two of them retreated into the coach.

Merliss jumped up when she saw them coming. Flood motioned for them to get as far from the other passengers as possible before they spoke. They took refuge in the double seat at the far end of the car. In spite of knees that were feeling a little shaky, Flood stood while the other two sat. McGinnis briefed his niece on the fight while Flood took the knife from his coat pocket and examined it. The blade was about eight inches long and free of any trace of blood. It had a brass cross guard and ivory grip. The handle contained a carved image, and Flood had to hold it at an angle to the light to make out the figure. "Looks like two men riding double on a horse," he remarked, handing the knife over to the professor.

McGinnis gave it a close inspection. "That's a symbol of the early Templars. You can still see it engraved on some of their old castles. It's meant to show both their poverty and their charity."

"From poverty and charity to greed and murder," Flood commented. He took the knife and slipped it into his pocket as he saw the conductor swinging himself along the aisle by the seat backs.

"Memphis! Next stop, Memphis! Twenty minutes to Memphis!" He continued on through to the next car.

"There may be more than one of these killers aboard," Flood said, lowering his voice. "We need to be certain we shake them off our trail. Instead of getting a through ticket at Memphis to go on West, we'll get another train north to Saint Louis."

"Why, in the name of Rumpelstiltskin, would we do that?" McGinnis snapped, apparently fully recovered from his fright.

Maybe the man didn't have enough sense to be afraid, Flood thought.

"He just told you, Uncle Mac," Merliss said patiently. "We can always head south later."

"Exactly," Flood said. "The main thing right now is to throw off any pursuit. When a jack rabbit is fleeing from a coyote, he doesn't just run in a straight line. No, he zigzags so sharply that the bigger animal can't cut as fast and loses ground. We will zig and zag and, hopefully, throw them off our tail for good." He tried to give them an encouraging smile, knowing he had to be the strong one here, but his knees were so weak, he had to brace himself up by the back of the seat. "When we reach Saint Louis, we'll get some different clothes, hats, maybe a couple of false beards. We don't know who these men are, or where they are, so we can't take any chances. The only ones we've seen who can be identified so far have been those in hauberks and helmets."

Merliss shivered and wrapped her arms around herself. "It's all so bizarre. Like I'm caught up in some ridiculous nightmare."

Flood had an urge to put his arm around her shoulders and give her a reassuring hug, but hesitated. How would she take it? He felt he didn't know her well enough, and let the moment pass.

"I'll have to telegraph my school in New Orleans that I

won't be back," Merliss lamented. "I'll be fired for not giving notice. Maybe blacklisted from other teaching positions. And my things at the boarding house in Nashville. . . ."

"Wire the boarding house three day's rent and tell them to hold your luggage," McGinnis said shortly. "Is there anything there you can't part with?"

"Not really," she replied slowly, "except my nice leather grip and a tortoise shell mirror and brush set that belonged to Mother. . . ."

"You'll get it all back," McGinnis said impatiently, waving his hand. "But both of you have got to start looking at the bigger picture. When we get our hands on this treasure, you'll forget all about any other possessions."

The man's cockiness irritated Flood who said: "Do you know *exactly* where this treasure is located? Can you go right to it?"

The professor slitted his eyes until they looked like blue pinpoints. "I can find it!" he snapped.

That's not what I asked, Flood thought, but clamped his mouth shut and slid into the vacant seat in front of them.

Just in case anyone might be watching the ticket agent in Memphis, they paid a porter at the dépôt to buy them three one-way Pullman tickets to St. Louis. The overnight train for the Missouri city pulled out within the hour. As they rolled over the Mississippi River bridge and started north, a spring storm swept down out of the west.

As Flood watched the rain lashing at the dark windows, he wondered if anyone had yet missed the lone man he'd hurled off the train. Was the man overdue for a report to someone else? Was there anyone at Memphis who was to meet him? Had the Templar been severely injured or killed in his fall from the speeding train?

Flood stripped down to his underwear and fell, exhausted, into the bunk knowing there was no way of answering these questions now. All they could do was to move fast in a zigzag pattern and hope to elude the coyote.

Chapter Six

Great Bend, Kansas
May, 1898

"By the shifting sands of the Sahara that damned train riding is thirsty work! I need something to cut the dust out of my throat," Roddy McGinnis croaked as he eyed the signboard hanging over the sidewalk a half block away that proclaimed the establishment within as the **Cock & Bull**.

The train they'd just vacated was chuffing away from the small dépôt at Great Bend, Kansas, leaving the pale afternoon sky stained with acrid coal smoke. It was four days later and the three weary travelers had unanimously voted to interrupt their flight for a day or two, to catch their breath and firm up their plans.

As they stepped out into the dusty main street, Flood was grateful to have something solid and unmoving beneath his feet for a change. He wondered how people who took long sea voyages were able to stand constant motion for months.

The professor, who still wore the false white whiskers glued to his face, was eyeing the saloon sign and licking his lips.

"Let's get checked into a hotel first," Merliss urged. "I really need to freshen up and get out of these clothes." She nodded at The Pioneer Hotel just across the street from the dépôt.

Grumbling under his breath, McGinnis followed them

across to the hotel, a small pack slung over one shoulder that contained a change of clothing and his precious leather packet of papers and notes.

McGinnis rented two adjacent rooms for the night and signed the register for them as Mary Jenson and Jethro Pollard, and for himself Jonathan Edwards.

As they carried their sparse luggage to their upstairs rooms, Flood finally began to relax. They had not seen or heard of any Templars since they'd boarded the overnight train to St. Louis. There, during the eight hours between trains, McGinnis had cashed a draft on his bank in Chicago. Flood didn't see the amount, but noticed the professor later stuffing a folded wad of bills into the top of his ankle-high boot.

Merliss still had some of her own money and insisted on using it to buy herself some appropriate traveling clothes, a few personal items, and a carpetbag to carry them in. Flood and McGinnis had also augmented their wardrobe, including hats and, in a theatrical shop, had obtained a fake mustache and white beard. The shopkeeper had helped them glue on the whiskers and proudly proclaimed that no one more than two feet away could tell it wasn't growing from their faces.

A local westbound had jolted them for the better part of forty-eight hours through the Missouri hills, stopping at every village and hamlet and being sidetracked by express trains and fast freights. Finally they'd had enough and got off halfway across the Kansas plains. A sense of security from pursuit and ambush had crept into Flood's bones with each peaceful day, and the constant fear of the mysterious Templars had begun to fade. He no longer felt the eyes of strangers on him in a crowd, and had relaxed into a state of quiet caution. In the lobby of the hotel he noticed two black-suited men, one wearing a bowler, the other a sweat-stained felt hat, pushed back on his head. One was jotting something in a small notebook. As Flood passed them, he caught a few words of their conversation and guessed they were reporters in town to cover the visit of some celebrity. Who could it be? He'd hoped Great Bend was a place of quiet anonymity.

There was one bathroom with a tub on each floor of the three-story hotel, and the men waited in their room for Merliss to bathe and dress. About an hour later, as the sun was setting, they met in the lobby.

"By the hairy whores of Babylon, I'm glad to be rid of that beard!" McGinnis exclaimed, rubbing his blotched face where he'd soaked and scrubbed the glue off, using the pitcher and basin in their room. Neither man had taken the time to shave and still wore about four day's growth of stubble.

"Merliss, you look fresh as a prairie breeze," Flood commented, thinking that her eyes would dull the blue of morning glories. She wore a divided riding skirt and boots and a white shirtwaist.

"Thank you, kind sir," she smiled, giving him a mock curtsy. "Would you gentlemen care to accompany a lady to supper? I noticed a steakhouse a couple of doors down advertising fresh Kansas beef."

"You two go ahead," McGinnis growled. "I've got a thirst you could scrape off the back of m' tongue."

Flood glanced at Merliss, wondering if she would object to letting her uncle out of her sight in a saloon.

"We'll join you later," she said brightly.

"Capital idea!" McGinnis beamed, leading them out of the lobby into the late afternoon sunshine. Except for the white stubble on his chapped face, the professor looked almost dapper in his black pants, herringbone tweed jacket, and new black hat that kept the unruly white hair in place.

"Don't be long." The professor nodded to them and strode away with a long, loose-limbed stride toward the Cock & Bull on the corner.

"There's no way I can keep him from drinking if he's bound to do it," she said as they entered the crowded café and found a small table. "He was my guardian, and not the other way around. I just didn't want him to endanger all of us by getting drunk on the train."

A white-aproned waiter took their order.

"Do you have any idea where Uncle Mac is going?" she inquired beneath the hum of voices and the clanking of glassware.

"He mentioned New Mexico, but that's a big territory. I thought maybe he'd confided in you, since you're family."

She laughed shortly. "I wish that were the case. The first I knew about all this was when I found you two in Nashville."

"How long since you'd seen him before that?"

"About a year. We keep in touch by letter."

"But you knew nothing about his work, or his ideas concerning the current existence of the Templars and their treasure?"

She shook her head. "I was just going to meet him at the conference for a short holiday."

Flood found himself losing his train of thought as he stared at those blue-green eyes so close across the table. He jerked his attention away and looked around the room. A stuffed antelope head was mounted on the wall. Two men were shooting pool in an adjoining room. The majority of the supper patrons appeared to be ranchers or laborers. He saw no one who remotely resembled what he would suspect as a Templar.

He brushed away two flies that had landed to inspect a stain on their table. He could imagine what this place would be like when the weather got warmer. "Do you intend to see this thing through to the end?" he asked her.

She shrugged. "I suppose so. Except for his older sister in southern Illinois who's in bad health, I'm the only family he's got. Going with him will cost my job, but that can't be helped."

"Has he always been like this?"

"How? Eccentric?"

"Yeah."

"Oh, yes. Ever since I can remember, at least. But, because I grew up with him, his behavior didn't seem strange to me."

"Let me ask you something." He fixed her with a steady gaze. "Do you really believe this Templar treasure exists? And, if so, that he actually knows how to find it? Or is he like some crazy prospector who has himself convinced that the mother lode is always just over the next hill?"

She didn't reply immediately, and Flood thought he detected a hesitancy, or doubt, on her face. Finally she looked up and said: "I've never known my uncle to lie. Some of his quirky ideas and theories that I've discounted in the past have actually turned out to be true. That's probably the reason he has such respect among his colleagues."

"Then you do believe him?"

She held up her hand. "I didn't say that."

"Then just what are you saying?" Flood tried to keep the impatience out of his voice. Here was a sensible person he could talk to candidly, so he'd better not alienate her. McGinnis had already paid him for a week's work, and the amount was most generous, so what did it really matter if this venture were only a journey to nowhere? At the moment he had no other prospects for employment.

"He believes in the treasure," Merliss said, choosing her words carefully.

73

"A lot of people believed in the Holy Grail over the centuries, but it's never been found," Flood said, pressing her. "Do you honestly, in your heart, as an intelligent woman, believe in this treasure? Think of yourself as unrelated to him and give me an honest answer."

"Yes, I believe in it," she replied simply. "But I have no proof. I'm taking it on faith in his scholarship. Does that answer your question?"

He nodded. "And you think those coded notes of his that look like hieroglyphics contain the directions for finding it?"

"He claims they do. Again, I have to take him at his word."

Just then the waiter arrived with their food, and they were silent for several seconds as they proceeded to eat.

"If you believe in him, then I believe in him," Flood said around a mouthful of steak.

"Well, as he used to be fond of quoting Abraham Lincoln . . . 'If the end brings me out right, then what is said against me won't amount to anything. If the end brings me out wrong, ten angels swearing I was right would make no difference.' "

Flood relaxed into a laugh. "He's a character, all right. I think I'll stay and see this hand played out just to find out who wins the pot."

"Dealing with Uncle Mac, you won't get bored, I can assure you." She smiled.

One of her infrequent smiles just added to the glory of those eyes. Flood wondered how her male students could concentrate.

"Do you teach in a female academy?"

"No. What made you think that? It's a public secondary school. Mostly freshmen and sophomores."

"I'd bet every one of the boys is in love with you."

"Adolescent infatuation is one of the hazards of the job,"

she laughed. "What about you? Have you ever worked as a bodyguard before?"

He shook his head and took a sip of coffee. "I've done a little of everything else and not much of anything. But this job is certainly different . . . even from pulling guard duty in the cavalry. I can imagine how some of the U.S. Secret Service men feel. This is very frustrating, knowing that the person I'm trying to protect can't be isolated. And the enemy can't be identified until it's too late." He shook his head. "If someone wants him bad enough, they'll get him in spite of my constant vigilance, just like an assassin got President Garfield back in 'Eighty-One."

"I'm glad he got rid of those fake whiskers," she said. "And that mustache looked ridiculous on you. Detracted from a most handsome face."

He acknowledged the compliment with a nod. "Well, I figured we were safe enough by now. And, speaking of whiskers," he added, " I need a shave."

"Yes, you do," she said, taking a bite of potatoes. "Don't monks grow beards and shave their heads?"

"You're probably thinking of Greek Orthodox monks you may have seen in pictures. Some of the older monks at my monastery still wear beards, but most of the younger ones shave about twice a month . . . just often enough to look scruffy most of the time. And tonsured hair is still a common practice."

She gave him an appraising look. "Somehow, I can't picture you as a monk."

"Monks are something of an anomaly in modern America," he evaded.

"Isn't it like being on some kind of permanent religious retreat?" she asked.

"I guess you could look at it that way."

"How did it feel, living with a bunch of saints?"

He snorted a laugh. "That's like asking you what it was like to teach a bunch of perfectly behaved students. Monks are just a group of men who want to get closer to God through contemplation, work, and prayer in a setting that's away from the distractions of the outside world. You can bet they all bring their personal faults and foibles with them."

"Will you go back there when this is over?"

Flood felt his throat constrict and laid his fork down, covering his discomfort by wiping his mouth with a napkin. "I have a feeling, when this is over, all our lives will be changed completely. Who can say? I have no plans in that direction."

She nodded, shoving her plate aside and taking up a spoon to eat her chocolate pudding.

They fell silent, finishing their supper, but her questions about monasticism had again brought the whole problem of violence and warfare to Flood's mind. Maybe one day, after he'd known her longer, he'd plumb her feelings and beliefs on this subject. Meanwhile, it would have to remain a personal struggle. He'd been born during the War Between the States, so he'd not had to face conscription, or the ridicule of others for not enlisting. But he'd enlisted in the cavalry at age nineteen only for the adventure of it and had faced hostile action twice against Mescalero Apaches. Now the United States regulars and volunteers were about to invade Cuba to fight the Spanish. Even if he'd believed in the cause, he would not have volunteered since it seemed every young blood in the country who wanted to make a name for himself or impress the home folks was trying to be first in line to sign up for a uniform and rifle.

He recalled that St. Bernard of Clairvaux had used mostly quotes from the Old Testament to justify the Knights Templar in their holy war against the infidel Moslems. But then, the Old Testament God had not hesitated to use fire and sword to smite the enemies of His chosen people. "An eye for an eye" the Jews believed. Whereas, the God of the New Testament, in the form of Jesus Christ, appeared to be just the opposite—love thy neighbor, do good to those who hurt you. Was this the same God talking? In the fundamental theology he'd been taught, God was One and could not contradict Himself. Aye, there was the rub, as Hamlet might have put it. Perhaps killing was a matter of divine policy—not an inherent evil. If God created life, He certainly had the option to destroy it, if He chose. It only remained for man to obey—whether God commanded him to fight, or to love his enemy. But without divine intervention, knowing God's will in particular circumstances was the problem. Flood assumed that he just couldn't see the whole picture. But for the sake of his own peace of mind, he'd have to keep looking for the missing pieces of the puzzle. In the meantime, he'd continue doing what seemed best at the moment with no thought of any ideological standard. He wondered again about the man he'd thrown from the train and the man in chain mail he'd shot on the Kentucky road. Were they still alive?

"Marc? Marc!"

His attention was rudely jerked back to his beautiful dinner companion.

"Are you all right?" she asked, concern in her face. "You seem to have left me for a while there."

"Just thinking that a little knowledge is a dangerous and frustrating thing."

"Something you'd like to get off your mind?" she asked, with unusual perception. "I'm told I have a pretty good ear."

He tried to give her an off-hand smile. "Maybe later. When we have more time. Right now, if you're finished, I think we'd better go check on your uncle."

The Cock & Bull had apparently made some pretensions at being an English public house when it was newer. Besides the name, about all that was left were a dark mahogany bar and woodwork, along with a dusty painting of Queen Victoria over the back-bar, facing a portrait of President William McKinley.

All this Flood took in at a glance as they entered. Because of the warm evening, the door had been left open, apparently in defiance of the law or in open co-operation with the same. Only the batwing doors partially screened off the view from the sidewalk.

Before Flood's eyes adjusted to the interior dimness, he heard McGinnis's voice.

"Uncle Mac!" Merliss said, hurrying toward the professor who was leaning on the far end of the bar, haranguing the mustachioed bartender. Flood caught a few words of the monologue that had something to do with the sexual habits of certain medieval knights.

"That's all very interesting, but I've got to wait on these customers," the bartender cut in, moving toward Flood and leaving the garrulous McGinnis still talking. Then, seeing Merliss more clearly, he said firmly: "We don't serve women in here."

"Hell, man, this is almost the Twentieth Century," Flood said. "What kind of an attitude is that?"

"I don't know where you're from, mister, but that's the way we do things around here. Kansas is a dry state, but as long as we don't cause any trouble, the law looks the other way. We found out from experience that women in a saloon are trouble. Men get t' fightin' over 'em and all that. Sure as some ruckus starts, the prohibitionists will have the sheriff enforce the law and shut us down."

Flood felt a warning pinch on his arm from Merliss. "She's with me," Flood continued in a milder tone. "We're just coming in to pick up her uncle over there." He nodded at McGinnis who was still propped against the bar, muttering to himself.

"In that case, you're welcome. I'll even give you a free drink if you'll take him outta here before I have to put him out for being drunk. He startin' to get loud and abusive. Besides that, he's talking my ears off about some damn' soldiers from olden times. Who is that old guy, anyway?"

"Roddy McGinnis," Merliss said.

Flood shot her a warning glance, but it was too late. Maybe the bartender wouldn't remember, since the name obviously meant nothing to him.

"He just likes to talk when he's drinking," Merliss hurried on, a little flustered.

"That's an understatement, lady."

"Are you serious about that offer of a free drink?" Flood asked.

"One drink each, as long as you get him out of here as soon as you finish."

"I'll have a beer."

The bartender nodded and looked expectantly at Merliss.

"Red wine of some kind, if you have it."

The bartender went to fill the orders as they approached McGinnis.

"Uncle Mac. . . ."

Flood held up his hand and stepped in front of her. "Professor, let's have a drink . . . over here at this table. Sit down. We need to make some plans for tomorrow." He reached behind McGinnis to the free lunch set out on the end of the bar. He sliced off a hunk of the crusty bread, a piece of crumbling yellow cheese, and dipped a pickled egg out of a stone jar and put them on a plate.

"Thought you just ate," McGinnis said.

"This is for you."

"Hell, I don't need that."

"Yes, you do," Flood said firmly. He guided the older man to a chair at a nearby table with Merliss following, carrying the beer and her glass of wine.

Flood was aware of the stares of the dozen or so men in the room, but talked quietly to keep from drawing any more attention to them. "Here, get some of this food inside you," he urged.

The old man picked at the cheese.

Merliss sipped her wine, as the rest of the patrons—men dressed mostly as ranchers, farmers, and railroad section hands—began to drag their attention back from her to their own drinks and card games. A low hum of conversation resumed.

Flood succeeded in persuading the professor to eat, even though McGinnis was grumbling and complaining that his whisky glass was empty. Flood got a cup of strong black coffee from the bartender for McGinnis to wash down the food. As he finally began to eat, the professor's appetite seemed to pick up.

Flood sat quietly, hearing snatches of conversation from the adjoining table. Two middle-aged men were talking about their sons volunteering to fight in Cuba. It seemed they had ridden off that day for Wichita to join some volunteer company and then entrain for San Antonio. Talk of the war was everywhere. Even a newspaper the idle bartender was reading bore headlines designed to stir up the readers against the Spanish in Cuba. Flood could read the large black headlines from where he sat.

As the food and coffee began to do their restorative work,

the professor became more animated. He sat back in his chair and sighed. "By the belly of Friar Tuck, I didn't know I was that hungry!"

"We're all pretty tired, Uncle Mac," Merliss said.

"And that whisky on an empty stomach hit you pretty hard," Flood added. "Why don't we go back to the hotel and get a good night's sleep?" He didn't mention the agreement he'd made with the bartender. He lowered his voice. "You don't want to leave your papers unguarded for too long." He knew McGinnis had thrust the leather packet under his mattress, but Flood was using any excuse to get him outside.

Flood tipped up his glass to drain his beer, and suddenly the batwing doors flew open and a big, black-clad figure burst in, followed by three smaller ones. They'd marched halfway to the bar before Flood realized they were women. All of them were clad from chin to toes in black dresses and wore hats of the same color.

The one in the lead slammed the flat of her hand down on the bar with a bang that drew every eye in the room to her. "I'm Carry A. Nation!" she thundered in the voice of a street preacher. "These ladies and I represent the Women's Christian Temperance Union and all the decent, God-fearing people of Kansas."

The bartender had edged back as far as he could and was glancing about him, either for a means of escape or a weapon.

"Liquor is the corrupting influence of mankind, and we have come to shut down this illegal den of iniquity." She turned and swept her gaze over the room, her eyes beady black behind the lenses of wire-rimmed spectacles. "These men should be home with their wives. Yet, here they sit, spending their hard-earned money, taking the bread out of the mouths of their children. Yes, they waste time here, besotting their senses, gambling, and"—her eyes fell on Merliss

McGinnis—"and whoring!"

"What?" Merliss looked stunned. "Who are you calling a whore, you old busybody?" she cried, her face flaming.

Carry Nation stood, triumphantly, a hand on one ample hip, as if daring anyone to oppose her. He broad face was illuminated by the yellow light of the overhead coal-oil lamp.

Flood had read about the escapades of this single-minded crusader, but never thought he'd see her in the flesh. And flesh there was—she was at least six feet tall in her high-top, lace-up shoes, and righteous wrath quivered from every one of her two-hundred pounds. Her broad face featured a wide, pug nose and full lips, downturned at the corners as if she'd just bitten into a stalk of rhubarb.

Flood glanced at McGinnis whose mouth had fallen open at this apparition. "By the mirror of Venus, is that a creature of the female race?" the professor croaked. His voice carried in the suddenly quiet room. "I've seen black pustules of plague that were handsomer than that!"

A big, red-faced rancher at the next table guffawed, and the rest of the men joined in the general hilarity. "They been digging up mastodon bones hereabouts," the rancher continued, pushing back his broad hat. "Do you reckon they accidentally came upon a live one that got away from them?"

Ridicule must have been something, besides alcohol, that this woman could not tolerate. At some signal from her, the three other women drew out short bats they'd been hiding in the folds of their voluminous skirts and began swinging at everything in reach. Carry Nation herself produced her signature hatchet and brought it down on the table nearest her. The four men at the table scattered, overturning chairs in their haste as the hatchet split the round tabletop completely across.

The bartender fled as the other three women marched

behind the bar and began smashing the rows of bottles on the shelves.

"Somebody stop her!" a man yelled over the noise of crashing glass.

Flood grabbed Merliss by the arm, and the three of them jumped out of the way as the avenging angel drew near, kicking over tables in her path and scattering cards and poker chips.

"The Lord drove the money-changers from the Temple!" she cried. "The righteous shall prevail!"

"In case you haven't noticed, this ain't no temple, lady!" a man shouted above the uproar.

"Down with demon rum!" one of the other women yelled, taking a full swing at a row of bottles and sending a shower of glass and liquor across the bar onto the floor.

"What's wrong with these men?" McGinnis grated. "Why don't they fight back?"

Two well-aimed swings at the back-bar mirror and it dissolved in a spangle of silver shards. The portrait of Queen Victoria bounced down from the wall, breaking its frame.

"Chivalry!" Flood shouted back in reply. "These men never hit a lady!"

"Lady, my ass!" he howled. "I've seen mogul locomotives more lady-like!"

"Destroy this devil's brew!" Nation bellowed, following her own advice with a massive blow at a keg behind the bar. The hatchet split the end of the wooden keg and beer spewed out in a sheet of foam, soaking the front of her dress.

Flood heard a deep-throated growl and turned in time to see McGinnis snatch up the pickled eggs and hurl them, point-blank. The crock jar caught Nation fully in the face, and she staggered back, glasses and hat askew. Beer and vinegar drenched her broad front, running down her face as ten-

83

drils of hair began to come loose from the tight bun on her head. A trickle of blood oozed from one nostril as she stood, glassy-eyed and swaying slightly, like some massive tower about to fall.

"Call the law!" someone yelled. "Throw the bitches out!"

"No! Don't call the sheriff!" the bartender shouted, running out from the back and waving his arms. "He'll close us down. This is a dry state!"

"Let's get out of here!" Flood got Merliss by the hand and hustled her through the wreckage. He pushed her through the swinging doors and looked back, but McGinnis was not right behind him as he had expected.

"You little weasel!" Nation roared, suddenly recovering and rolling her corset-laced bulk over the top of the bar. She landed on her feet and lunged at the lean professor. But the boiled eggs on the floor squished from under her feet at the same instant that McGinnis sprang out of the way and thrust out a bony leg to trip her. She fell like an axed oak, splintering one of the few remaining chairs.

"Wow! You'd think with all that exercise, the old hippo would lose some weight!" McGinnis piped, bounding past Flood into the street. "By a cuckold's horns, I haven't had that much fun since I was digging the ruins of Acre . . . and plowing a local Jezebel!"

Merliss looked at Flood and rolled her eyes in apparent resignation. They hurried down the street, following the old man.

They passed the two reporters, one snapping photographs and the other furiously scribbling in a notebook.

"By the smeared ink of the Magna Carta, she'll be stumping for women's suffrage next!" the professor cried as he disappeared into the hotel lobby.

Chapter Seven

Omaha, Nebraska
May, 1898

"They lost him. Four attempts, and all we have to show for it is a man with a bullet in his shoulder, another with a collar bone and arm broken from being thrown from a train, and McGinnis's niece who got away to warn him, leaving our man red-faced and bare-assed!"

Daniel Helverson cringed at the icy tone of Thomas D'Arcy's voice. D'Arcy let the curtain fall and turned from the big front window to face Helverson who stood uneasily in the middle of the living room, waiting for a reprimand. Helverson knew that he was in no way involved in these abortive attempts at silencing the threat of the Chicago professor. Yet he felt the wrath emanating from the Grand Master of the Western Knights Templar who stood before him.

D'Arcy remained silent while the grandfather clock in the corner ticked off several ominous seconds. Then the man in the dark suit took a deep breath, and some of the tension seemed to go out of him. He rubbed a hand over his neatly trimmed white beard. "One skinny old professor . . . ," he began thoughtfully. "Apparently harder to kill than a flat tick. But ships have been sunk by wood-boring worms, and deadly microscopic organisms can eventually kill the strongest ox. This man must be dealt with, or he could expose and bring down our entire organization. Maybe the boys should have used modern weapons instead of trying to terrorize him with all those medieval trappings."

Helverson shifted his weight, turning his hat nervously in his hands as D'Arcy vented his frustration. Helverson had faced violent men before, and he instinctively knew that D'Arcy was not himself a violent person. Helverson knew this flinty, sixty-year old man would not have risen to the position of a vice-president of the Union Pacific Railroad or been secretly elected Grand Master of the Knights Templar without a large dose of self-discipline.

D'Arcy had been Grand Master of the Western Knights Templar for only a week. The former Grand Master had been tried and executed by the ruling council for failure to eliminate Roddy McGinnis and obtain Peter Stirling's diary. Helverson had no doubt what his own fate would be if he failed in the mission he was about to be given.

He'd been summoned by cryptic telegram from his small ranch in Colorado to a personal meeting with the Grand Master. He'd arrived by Union Pacific this morning, checked into a hotel, and rented a horse to report directly to this house. It was only the most urgent business that required a personal interview with the Grand Master. He'd been in this house four times before, and each time he had been assigned to remove a dangerous enemy of the order.

Helverson had been a Western Knight Templar for ten years and, on several occasions, had been entrusted with enforcing the will of its leaders. Each time he'd been successful, and his superiors began to trust him with more and more dangerous and responsible assignments. He had gained a reputation within the order as a man who could get things done. At thirty, he was still a young man and had hopes of eventually rising to a higher position in the order.

"Word has reached me from our man at the University of

Chicago that McGinnis has the directions to the treasure written down," D'Arcy continued. "If he has transferred these directions to anyone else, or left them in a safety deposit box somewhere, then we have to move quickly. But I also understand this Roddy McGinnis is a very prideful individual . . . about half-cracked, my contact tells me. A man who would not trust his secret to *anyone* until he was ready to spring it on the world. A man who would rather take the secret to his grave than share it with anyone else."

Helverson waited patiently for the older man to get to the point of this meeting. Patience was one thing he had in abundance—patience and loyalty—the two virtues he had demonstrated in his proud ten years as a knight.

"Helverson," D'Arcy continued, less in the manner of a superior, "since that treasure was brought to the New World in the Fifteen Hundreds, and Peter Stirling died without revealing its location, it has been lost to our order. We don't want to go down in history as the generation that had a chance to recover the treasure, but failed. We must take whatever measures necessary to ensure that does not happen."

D'Arcy was striding back and forth on the carpeted floor, thumbs hooked in his vest pockets. "The Templars are a proud old order of warrior monks who have carefully guarded many sacred relics," he continued. "Did you know," he asked, turning to Helverson, "that our forebears had possession of what is now known as the Shroud of Turin for about a hundred and fifty years after the first crusade?"

"No, I didn't." Helverson was duly impressed.

"But to get to practicalities. . . ." He paused, as if organizing his thoughts. "Apparently McGinnis is traveling with a bodyguard, and he is the one who has frustrated our attempts to get to the professor. I'm assigning you the task of finding and neutralizing this McGinnis. How you do it is your business. If you find it necessary to kill him, it would be better if you could make it look like an accident, or the result of a random armed robbery."

This professor was another man who could be looked upon as an infidel of old. He was the enemy of both God and His soldiers, the Knights Templar. Not only was eliminating McGinnis justified, Helverson reasoned, but it would bring glory upon himself as a warrior for Christ.

D'Arcy came closer and put a hand on Helverson's shoulder in an almost fatherly manner. "There is a lot riding on you. But you've earned the trust and confidence of all of us. If there's anything further you need, you know how to contact me." He picked up a folded copy of the Omaha *Herald* from the horsehair sofa and pointed to an article. "This might give you a place to start. It's the last clue we have as to the whereabouts of this professor and his bodyguard."

Helverson took the paper and read the small headline on the column: **WCTU ATTACKS SALOON**. In smaller type just below it: **Carry Nation Chops Up Illicit Bar in Great Bend, Kansas**. Glancing quickly down the column, he read that a thin, white-haired drunk had counterattacked this prohibitionist with a crock jar and knocked her down before fleeing with a young man and woman. The bartender credited the older man, he identified as Roddy McGinnis, for helping to prevent the Cock & Bull from being completely destroyed by **these crazy prohibitionists who have no regard for other people's property**.

"That's our man," D'Arcy confirmed when Helverson looked up. "That attack happened two days ago. At least, it will give you a place to start." He pulled a gold watch from his vest pocket and popped open the case. "I have to get down to the office for a meeting. Report back to me by the usual coded telegram when you have something. You're under no time constraints, but I would suggest that speed is your ally. If you can somehow make this McGinnis look like a fool and discredit him, fine. If not, either get his notes, or let him lead you to the treasure before destroying him. Don't let anything stand in your way. If you need further help, contact me. But remember that I'm holding you responsible." He thrust out his hand, and Helverson was surprised at the strength of the older man's grip.

With those ominous parting words, he went out and closed the door behind him. Helverson, standing in the hallway, realized he was perspiring as he listened to the footsteps clumping down off the porch and saw the gray-suited figure striding up the street. Although a vice-president of the Union Pacific, the Grand Master chose to maintain a low profile and rode the streetcar to work from this two-story frame house about three miles from U.P. headquarters in downtown Omaha. Helverson wondered what went on inside this man's head. D'Arcy had never married and lived here alone with only a black servant for help and company. It was rumored that D'Arcy, years before, in a very solemn ceremony and following the original written Rule of the order, had taken the vows of poverty, chastity, and obedience when he was made a knight. All the money he earned, except for a few living expenses, was funneled into the order. Even this house where he had met with D'Arcy was owned by the Knights Templar. Helverson stared after the newly elected Grand Master long after he was out of sight. The big clock ticked monotonously in the silence of the great house with its dark furniture and heavy drapes. A great weight had been placed on his shoulders—the weight of almost eight hundred years of history and tradition. And now it was up to him to maintain the secrecy of that society—and to recover the ancient treasure. An awesome responsibility. His stomach was tense, but he welcomed the challenge. It was similar to a feeling he used to get as a member of the University of Michigan football squad just before every big game—before the brutal hitting began and the screams of the spectators faded from his consciousness. He'd suffered several severe concussions, but a blinding headache now and then was his only reminder of those injuries. Having been reared by Danish parents on a Minnesota farm, he was inured to pain and hardship. A big-boned six feet, one inch, two-hundred and ten pounds, he knew he still had the physical equipment to withstand an inordinate amount of punishment.

He wiped the sheen of perspiration from his face and put on his hat.

The black servant glided noiselessly down the hallway to open the front door for him. "Good day, sir."

Helverson, unused to such amenities, only nodded as he went out.

It was good to be outside, breathing the fragrance of the spring air as he went down off the porch into the warm sunshine. He untied his horse from the iron hitching post at the curb and swung into the saddle. He guided the animal down the street in the direction of his hotel, still thinking of the Western Knights Templar and all they stood for. To him, they were the only organization, besides the Church, that openly championed moral values. And it was his job to oppose anyone or anything that was an enemy of the Templars. That included justifiable homicide against the sworn enemies of the order. The treasure would go a long way toward helping establish world peace and order under the New Holy Roman Empire.

He flexed his shoulders and felt the tension in his powerful muscles. He consciously tried to relax, focusing on the balmy air that was like a light, rare wine. His thoughts jumped ahead to this Professor McGinnis. If he could get his hands on that slippery little devil, it would be like wringing the neck of a chicken. But this bodyguard—he might be a different story, a worthy adversary. *Greater love than this, no man has, than he lay down his life for his friends.* If he were somehow killed in defending the Templars—a very remote possibility—he was confident of the reward of heaven. And no one could fight with more confidence than when he had right on his side.

Chapter Eight

Santa Fé
May, 1898

"Where'd you find *him?*" Marc Flood asked quietly. He pulled Roddy McGinnis aside and nodded toward a muscular, brown-haired young man lounging a few yards away under the roofed walkway that ran along the front of the adobe Governor's Palace.

"I met him in a *cantina* over there when I was having a dr . . . uh . . . lunch. He's a guide."

"Uncle Mac, he doesn't look like a guide," Merliss said, her tone dubious.

"By the Pillars of Hercules, what is a guide supposed to look like?" the professor rasped. "He's a strapping lad. Claims to know the area west of here very well and. . . ."

"And he just happened to be available?" Flood couldn't keep the sarcasm out of his voice.

"No. Yes. Well, he was in town to join a company of volunteers to go fight in Cuba, but he's willing to let that go and hire on to guide us. . . ."

"You didn't tell him what we're after?" Flood asked.

"No, of course not."

"Did you approach him, or the other way around?"

"I . . . uh . . . don't rightly remember. We just got to talking and. . . ."

Flood shook his head. From the smell of the professor,

he'd had more than a couple of drinks. Flood glanced at the young man who struck a match on one of the porch posts to light a slim cigar. He appeared unconcerned, relaxed. Yet, Flood felt, there was something about him that didn't seem quite right. Then it came to him. For a man who'd spent enough time outside to call himself a guide, this fellow was not tanned or weather-beaten. In this part of the country, at least a man's hands would have some evidence of the sun, even if he wore gloves part of the time in his work. And a hat, which he wasn't wearing at the moment, would shield only part of his face and neck from sun and windburn. Big and strong as he was, Flood thought, this man did not have the appearance of an outdoorsman. He also noted the canvas pants tucked into new brown boots and the collarless white shirt, stretching under the massive shoulders every time the man moved.

Flood absorbed all this in only a few seconds, then turned back to the professor.

"Now, look here," the white-haired McGinnis drew himself up to his full five-foot, eleven, "I'm still in charge of this expedition, and I'm paying the bills. You were hired to protect me, not to make judgments for me. So just do your part of the job and I'll do mine."

"I'm trying to," Flood replied under his breath as he edged the professor farther out of earshot toward the middle of the grassy area.

The two men stood silently for several seconds. A light breeze was moving the branches of the cottonwoods, throwing a dappled pattern of light and shadow across part of the ancient plaza.

Flood took a deep breath and faced McGinnis again. "Do your really think it's necessary to bring another person in on this? A perfect stranger?"

"You were a perfect stranger when we hooked up," McGinnis reminded him.

"Just damned lucky when you got *me,*" Flood said matter-of-factly, with no hint of pride. "Do you think this man will be satisfied with wages when he finds out there's treasure at the end of this quest?" Flood wasn't even sure he believed in the treasure himself, but this was not the time to consider that.

"Look here," the professor went on, "I must have a guide until we're close enough so that I can find it on my own. Peter Stirling's journal gives certain landmarks . . . trees that are, by now, long gone, mountains that are called by different names than any marked on modern maps. He named only the primary directions by the sun. The rivers in this part of the country have cut deeply into rock beds, so are probably still close to their old channels, but the distances are given in leagues, and a league could be anything from about two-and-a-half to four-and-a-half miles. So, you can see, this is going to take someone who knows the rivers and cañons and mountain ranges. We could wander around for weeks and possibly die of thirst out there without some sort of capable guide who is familiar with the region and the terrain."

Flood thought McGinnis's voice and delivery had reverted to that of a lecturing professor. "And if this man turns out to be a lying swindler or fortune hunter who knows nothing of the country?" he asked.

"Then you'll have to deal with him," McGinnis replied. "Unless you have some better suggestion?"

Flood thought the professor's personality seemed to grow a few more bristles after every drink. He looked at Merliss who'd remained mostly silent throughout this exchange. She nodded in agreement, and Flood acquiesced to her feminine judgment. "All right, we'll hire him." He turned to

McGinnis. "Introduce me."

As they moved back toward the would-be guide, Flood was impressed by the compact strength of the man.

"I'd like you to meet my two associates," the professor began. "This is my niece, Merliss McGinnis, and this is Marc Flood. Our new guide, Dan Helverson."

As Flood suspected, the man's hand was not callused, but there was bear-like strength behind that casual grip.

Then Helverson bowed slightly as he took Merliss's hand. "Miss," he murmured, giving her a look of more than routine interest.

Flood felt a sudden rush of jealousy and ground his teeth in anger at his own stupid reaction.

"As I was telling you earlier," McGinnis continued to Helverson, "one of my colleagues found a cliff dwelling of the Anasazi back in one of these cañons." He waved his hand in a vague westerly direction. "He claims to have discovered proof that these ancient Indians practiced a ritual of sacrifice that has never been known to exist among them. But my friend died before he was able to publish his report. I have his journal and his notes and hope to relocate this one particular cliff dwelling and confirm his findings." He smiled and went on in what Flood thought was a most convincing lie. "Of course, this is nothing earth-shaking . . . only an exciting discovery to one of my profession, and my two associates here who are studying under me. But it will give us more insight into these ancient people who left no written record of their passing."

"We'd like to leave by tomorrow," Flood interrupted. "Can you get an outfit together by then?"

Helverson nodded. "I believe so. Where are you staying?"

McGinnis pointed to the west end of the plaza. "Two doors down that side street."

"We'll meet you here at ten o'clock in the morning," Flood added.

"Do you need some advance money?" McGinnis queried.

Before Flood could put a stop to this, the muscular guide shook his head. "No. You can reimburse me. How long do we expect to be gone? There are more than a hundred cliff dwellings scattered over miles of that back country."

"We'll need supplies for at least three weeks," Flood said hastily. "Anything longer than that we'll come back to town. What do you think?"

Helverson nodded thoughtfully. "I don't know how far we'll be going, but we should be able to cover a good bit of territory in three weeks. I'll be off, then, and meet you back here in the morning, ready to go. If I run into any problems, I'll stop by your hotel." He nodded, raked his blue eyes across Merliss, and turned away, tossing his half-smoked cigar aside.

Flood had mixed feelings about this man, but held his silence. At least, Helverson had not asked for any money up front. A point in his favor. Maybe the man was legitimate, after all. "Well, that's done, for better or worse. Let's go get ourselves outfitted and then have something to eat."

"What kind of gun would you like?" Flood inquired of Merliss a few minutes later when they were inside a big, general merchandise emporium. McGinnis was across the room trying on some broad-brimmed hats.

"Gun?" She looked startled. "I don't know how to use a gun."

"I'll teach you."

"Why would I need one? This is Eighteen Ninety-Eight."

"And this is still the Territory of New Mexico. The railroad may have crossed it, and this town may be over two hundred years old, but that doesn't mean it's as civilized as New Orleans or Chicago. Besides, if anything happens, I don't want to be the only one armed."

"What about Uncle Mac?"

"Has he ever owned a gun?"

"Not that I know of."

"My point exactly."

She glanced at McGinnis, who was still occupied sorting through a stack of canvas pants. "What kind of trouble are you expecting? Other than rattlesnakes or cougars? The wild Indian tribes have been subdued. Or, is all this firepower to hunt fresh meat?"

"Just pick a gun, or I'll pick one for you."

A look of irritation crossed her face at his peremptory tone, but she turned to the glass case and studied the handguns displayed there. "Let me try that one."

The clerk handed her a .32 caliber Smith & Wesson pocket pistol with black rubber grips and nickel finish.

"This seems to fit my hand."

"Try thumbing back the hammer and squeezing the trigger. See if the spring is too strong."

She complied. "It's fine. But hitting something with it is a different matter."

"Don't worry. We'll work on that later. We'll take it," Flood said to the clerk. "Add two boxes of cartridges."

Then he picked out a Colt Lightning pump-action rifle that used the same cartridges as his Bisley.

Boots, hats, canvas riding pants, cotton shirts, waterproof ponchos, two-quart blanket-sided canteens, compass, field glasses, matches, and various personal items completed their shopping, and McGinnis mumbled under his breath when he saw the total cost the clerk added up on a pad of paper. But he paid with no comment, and they lugged their purchases back to their adobe hotel. The bright, ground floor room had a low ceiling with exposed beams and a beehive fireplace plastered one corner. They'd discovered the comfort of sleeping under a blanket at night when cool mountain air came sliding through the shutters.

When the three of them went to a nearby café, Flood picked up a newspaper to read as he ate. It was still full of news of the impending war. The troops had entrained from their training camp outside San Antonio and were on their way to Tampa, Florida where ships would transport them to Cuba for the invasion. Rallies of support were being held all along the route by crowds of flag-waving citizens. Americans had not been involved in a war since the last generation had fought each other on the bloody battlefields of their own country. The thirty-three years since the end of that conflict, Flood reflected, had seemed to obliterate the collective memory of its horror. The war hawks were screaming again, this time for the blood of the Spaniards who had their boots on the necks of the poor Cubans. There was no evidence of whether the explosion was accidental or deliberate. But, fueled by the yellow journalism of William Randolph Hearst and his newspaper empire, the cry—"Remember the *Maine*!"—seemed to be on everyone's lips. From the spread of stories on the front page, it seemed half the able-bodied men in America were marching toward Cuba and the other half were rushing the other way to find gold in Alaska.

Flood sighed and folded the newspaper open to an inside page where a photograph with a black background and a white image jumped out at him. The article underneath indicated that an Italian, Secondo Pia, had taken the first photographs of the Shroud of Turin and discovered, to his amazement, that the negative showed a detailed, positive image of a body bearing the marks of crucifixion. This startling discovery was triggering a rush by scholars and scientists to make a more thorough study of the shroud. Although no one could tell how the image had been formed on the cloth, and there was no proof it was actually the burial cloth of Jesus Christ, this strip of linen with its faint image had been the object of veneration by Christians for centuries. Flood felt a surge of his own faith as he stared at the picture of a bearded, naked man on the page. In spite of all the greed, lust, murder, and flawed policies pursued in the name of God over the centuries, here was something concrete to bolster his belief, and no amount of human folly could shake that.

He turned the paper to a back page where his eye fell on columns of ads for patent medicines, oil burners, therapeutic back supports, and all manner of products. Just below one of these advertisements was a small headline: **Famous Archaeologist Disappears**. He began scanning it, then said: "Listen to this!"

The professor and Merliss looked up from their food.

" 'A spokesman for the University of Chicago reported yesterday that Doctor Roddy McGinnis, internationally known archaeologist and historian, is missing,' " he read aloud. " 'According to Hiram Snell at the university, Professor McGinnis was on his way to Tennessee to deliver a lecture at a meeting of the International Society of Historical Anthropologists at Vanderbilt University. However, the professor never arrived, and no one has reported seeing him. A black buggy, thought to be his, was found burned on a rural road in southern Kentucky a few days later. A dead horse was nearby, but there was no sign of the professor. To compound the mystery, his niece, Miss Merliss McGinnis, was attacked by a man on the Vanderbilt campus the opening day of the conference. This apparent attempt to ravish was thwarted, and Miss McGinnis was last seen later that day riding a trolley toward downtown Nashville. Inquiries were made to officials at the conference when she failed to return to her teaching job in New Orleans, but to no avail. Apparently McGinnis enjoys being in the public eye, so it is very much out of character for him to vanish voluntarily. Although McGinnis is not known to have any enemies, foul play is suspected.' "

"By the rod of Aaron, it's nice to shake the powers on high! We've been missed!" McGinnis seemed positively delighted that someone cared enough to report him missing.

"Well, if any Templars read this, they won't have a clue as to our whereabouts, either," Merliss said. "Thank goodness."

Flood nodded. "It's just as well that you didn't contact your boarding house in Nashville or your school. We'll be safer if no one else knows who or where we are for now." He laid the paper aside and attacked his roast beef. "By the way," he said to McGinnis around a mouthful of food, "you never told me how this treasure wound up in the American Southwest. In the Fifteen Hundreds, this area was a wilderness with nothing but a lot of space and Indians. If I remember my history correctly, the Spanish explorers were just then sending expeditions up from Mexico."

"Right you are. And do you remember what they were seeking? They later planted a few settlers along the Río Grande Valley, but at first they weren't just out to explore for colonization or to convert the Indians. Why do you think they traveled horseback for hundreds of miles through an unknown land without turning back from this god-awful infinity of rocks and heat?" He arched his eyes at Flood as if quizzing a student. "I'll tell you why. They were gold hungry. They'd just overrun Mexico and Peru, and they thought all Indian kingdoms in the New World were fabulously rich. They were following rumors of the seven cities of Cibola . . . the cities of gold. Like a donkey after a carrot, they kept following those rumors. Of course, there was no such thing. But my research has convinced me that the basis of those rumors was the gold treasure of the Templars. Word spread far and wide among the Indians, most of whom had never seen the treasure, but the Spaniards were completely bamboozled by it, following every false lead and assurance of their Indian guides."

"Sounds logical," Flood nodded. "But if a few of the Indians actually knew where this treasure was, why didn't they take it themselves?"

"The only reason I can come up with is that this treasure was hidden a generation or so before the first Spaniards came, so the Indians who'd actually seen the treasure had died off, and the exact location had become blurred in their oral tradition. Remember, the Pueblo Indians of that time had use for gold only as trinkets and something to work into art objects. They didn't value it as wealth like the whites did, for its economic worth and rarity."

Flood took a sip of coffee and wiped his mouth with a napkin. "Another thing that's not clear to me is how this treasure got to so remote a place that long ago?"

"Merliss has not heard this story before, either," McGinnis said, glancing at his niece. "So let me start at the beginning. When the Moslems finally overran the town of Acre on the eastern coast of the Mediterranean in Twelve Ninety-One, a handful of Templars survived and escaped by sea, taking the treasure from their fortress to the island of Cyprus. And there it stayed until Thirteen Oh Seven. Then the French King and the Pope summoned Jacques de Molay, the Grand Master of the Knights Templar, to France on the pretext of planning the next crusade, but really with the intent of arresting all the Templars on false charges, disbanding the order, and taking their wealth. Jacques de Molay arrived in Paris in style, we're told. It required twelve horses to carry just the silver and gold, not counting the train that was packed with rich equipment and fancy silks and wearing apparel. He deposited these treasures in the Temple at Paris before going to see King Philip the Fair. Then all hell broke loose, and the next several years were nothing but arrests, charges in court, squabbles between the Pope and the King, tortures and forced confessions, burnings at the stake. At one point in all this, fifteen hundred to two thousand Templars, who had eluded capture, took refuge in the hills outside Lyons, during one of the trials. They had managed to get the treasure from the Temple in Paris and were willing to defend their order against its accusers either with sworn testimony or force of arms. But the official Knights Templar were doomed, and the treasure was smuggled out of France to Scotland where it was buried beneath a Templar church for about two hundred years. Then what follows I have only from the journal of Peter Stirling, who had now come on the scene. Stirling writes in his journal that, because of the danger of the treasure being discovered and confiscated from beneath the church, a loyal band of Templars stole it away by ship and sailed with it to the Gulf Coast. From the mouth of what we know as the Río Grande, they transported the treasure hundreds of miles up the Río Grande Valley. Just reading his journal makes my hair stand on end. Weeks of hard marching and searing weather, starvation, and fever. They encountered the Pueblo Indians before the Spaniards did, so the Indians didn't know what to make of them and avoided any close contact. Stirling's party tried to coax them closer to buy some food, but the Indians were wary . . . probably more afraid of the pack mules and horses than of the men, since they'd never seen such animals before. Somewhere off in a remote cañon to the west of the river, the white men located an abandoned cliff dwelling of the Anasazi to hide the treasure. Stirling named it the Stone Castle, but there's no such place name now. Stirling was the only survivor of this party to finally make it back to Scotland two years later. He was refused the wealth and honor he thought he deserved and vowed he'd never turn over his record of the treasure."

"Seems stupid for the Templars to kill him before they were able to extract the location of the treasure," Flood remarked.

"By the Hounds of Hell, these men were malicious, not clever! Stirling contracted a fever in prison and died. They didn't intend to kill him."

"Well, I think we've finally thrown them off our trail," Flood said, but with no real assurance. "At least for now," he added, wondering how much of his statement was wishful thinking, spoken only to reassure the man he was trying to protect.

With the impending trek on his mind, Flood slept poorly that night. By dawn he finally gave up the attempt to sleep. He rose, dressed quietly, and slipped out while the other two slept. He walked down the empty streets toward the twin towers of St. Francis Cathedral, a block off the plaza, and slipped in a side door to attend the six o'clock Mass. About fifteen or twenty people were there, most of them of Mexican blood. He was impressed by the reverence they showed, seemingly oblivious to everything except what was taking place on the altar, and their own private prayers. It was the first opportunity he'd had to attend Mass since he'd left the monastery, and it might be weeks before he had the opportunity again. He prayed fervently for divine protection in their quest, whether or not it resulted in finding the mythical treasure. He drew strength from his faith and felt calmer and more confident when he crossed the plaza to the hotel.

As Flood looked around, he could almost see armored Spanish soldiers of two hundred years before and the swarms of Indians from nearby Pueblos. Maybe he'd been delving too deeply into history lately, since it took no effort at all to visualize the distant past as if it were the present. Of course, fighting real assassins in armor certainly helped fire the imagination.

The crowd milling about the plaza consisted mostly of tourists from the East who had heeded the gaudy posters printed by the railroad. These advertisements urged everyone to visit the quaint adobe towns of the Southwest that had been the site of so much bloodshed during the Spanish conquest and the later revolt of the Pueblo Indians. Santa Fé had an especially long and colorful history as the terminus of the Santa Fé Trail during the years when hundreds of loaded freight wagons arrived here after a long trek across the plains. Now all that was gone, and only a few dozen Indians still hunkered in the shade, their ornate silverwork spread out on colorful blankets for inspection by white women in long dresses who wandered about, parasols protecting their complexions from the fierce desert sun.

McGinnis had just finished dressing when Flood entered their room, and he knocked on the door of the adjoining room. "Merliss, my dear, are you up?"

A few seconds later the door opened, and she appeared, dressed and ready to ride, carrying her wide-brimmed hat. Her black hair was swept back and fastened at the base of her neck. Flood intentionally turned a blind eye to her beauty this morning. From now on, he would force himself to look upon her as just another person in the expedition, something of a neuter, a sexless individual. He could not afford to think of her as a woman, especially not a beautiful, desirable one.

Until they returned from this wilderness journey, Flood must concentrate on the business at hand, watching and listening, using all his skill and strength to protect this strange professor.

By the time they'd finished a breakfast of tortillas, beans, eggs, and coffee, he was beginning to get the feeling that this was going to be a very trying trip. His premonition started to come true as soon as they saw Helverson an hour later in the plaza. In addition to the loaded pack mules and horses, they were greeted not only by Helverson but two other men, all armed with rifles.

"Who're they?" Flood demanded, indicating the two men.

"Packers. Figured it'd be a sight easier if I had some help," Helverson replied evenly.

"We hired *you*. If you can't do the job by yourself, we'll get someone else. There are only three of us. You do the guiding, and we'll help with the packing," Flood said shortly.

Helverson shrugged, then walked over and said something to his companions, rough-looking men in their twenties or early thirties, Flood guessed. They had a short conversation, while the three glanced at Flood a time or two. Finally they hefted their rifles and walked away. Flood let out an unconscious sigh of relief. At least now they would have only one man to watch.

Helverson turned back with no trace of a smile. "I took the liberty of choosing some mounts for all of us." He handed the reins of the first horse to Flood. "Let's get mounted and move out."

Flood had a knot in the pit of his stomach. Maybe eating beans for breakfast had done it, although he'd adjusted to a very plain, sparse fare in the monastery. He didn't want to admit that the feeling was really a premonition of disaster, and they were rushing to meet it.

Chapter Nine

On the Trail

Merliss McGinnis was a city girl and she knew it. She secretly hoped she could keep up and endure whatever hardships this marching and camping entailed. All her new attire—the divided riding skirt, the stiff new boots, the broad-brimmed hat—were not enough suddenly to transform her into an outdoorswoman. At least, she was not embarrassed by her lack of riding skill, as they rode out of the adobe town of Santa Fé and turned their faces to the west. She had learned to ride in college and had even done a little jumping, but she'd used a light, English saddle, and all the galloping and cantering and trotting had been on enclosed, level arenas and show rings. There had been no cross-country trips. Even though she hadn't ridden in years, her training came back quickly, and she liked the comfortable Mexican-style saddle she sat on the long-limbed roan.

She doubted Marc Flood was fooled by her altered appearance, but so far this first day he'd hardly looked her way. He appeared distracted by all the details of the trip, checking the supplies of food, blankets, spare horseshoes, and other gear packed on a mule in large leather bags he called *aparejos*. For some reason she didn't understand, these had been thrown over the top of a wooden packsaddle—maybe to protect the mule's back from chaffing. There was actually a string of three pack mules, in addition to their four saddle horses with their saddlebags stuffed full. Although only one of the mules carried anything, the professor had insisted they have three. "By the slippery slopes of Perdition, one of them might fall and break a leg or be bitten by a snake. We need at least two spares," he'd replied when Helverson questioned him about the extra expense. "Besides, I might find some artifacts I need to bring back."

More likely heavy treasure, she had thought. She smiled at her uncle's strange ways. In spite of his peculiarities, there was no doubt he was a brilliant man—and well-suited to the academic community. The only other environment where she could envision him thriving was in a science laboratory, conducting experiments.

She drifted out of her reverie and took a deep breath of the fresh air, savoring the tang of sage on the breeze. The four of them were riding single-file, now heading west by north, with Helverson in the lead. She followed her Uncle Mac, who was second in line. Bringing up the rear a few yards behind her was Marc Flood, leading the three pack mules.

Riding in line precluded most conversation, but she was just as glad of it, since it gave her time to be alone with her thoughts and time to enjoy the magnificent panorama before her. The early June sun was climbing toward its zenith, and she was grateful for the wide-brimmed hat that protected her face and eyes. In this dry land the fierce rays of the sun were not filtered by a moist atmosphere as they were in New Orleans. The horses' hoofs scuffed up puffs of fine, red dust. The earth around them was even redder than Georgia clay. The land gave way in the middle distance to a rolling, dun-colored terrain sprinkled with mesquite and various high-desert shrubs. Beyond that, rising to form a jagged line across the horizon, were purplish-blue mountains.

In spite of the heat of the sun, a pleasantly cool breeze

blew into their faces as they rode, so the bandanna she wore inside her open shirt collar was not uncomfortably warm. She would not have removed it in any case, since it served to conceal the red birthmark on the right side of her neck. She knew it was silly to be sensitive about it, but she'd never quite been able to put the stares and giggles of her childhood classmates behind her. And, over the years, she'd grown weary of explaining to new acquaintances that the blemish was not a burn scar or a fresh abrasion. She'd finally taken to wearing high-necked dresses and shirtwaists to conceal it. She didn't know if Marc Flood had seen it yet. If so, he'd been gentlemanly enough not to comment. She wondered why she would care what Flood thought about the birthmark or about her. She had to admit she was attracted to him. He had a pleasant personality, seemed intelligent, and, of course, was extremely handsome. This latter fact made her wary. In her experience, good-looking young men usually carried the baggage of conceit and arrogance, believing that every female was bound to swoon before them. So far, Flood had not exhibited any of this pride. She had known him only about two weeks, although it seemed much longer since they'd been together on trains and in hotels and cafés most of that time. And the fact that he'd been a monk puzzled her. She would have to penetrate beyond the chiseled façade, but here, she thought, was a man worth knowing.

What of this new guide, Dan Helverson? He looked to be about thirty, thick brown hair, with a scar on his square chin. He was bigger and more muscular than Flood and also handsome in a rugged sort of way. So far, he'd hardly said a word to her, except in greeting, so she might have to question her uncle about him when she got a chance before she did any investigating on her own. She had always been very open with men of her own generation, but the frightening experience at

Vanderbilt had made her a lot more cautious about conversing with strange men, unless she was in a completely safe environment. And, as long as they were on this trek, she had the protection of Flood and Uncle Mac. Flood had insisted she buy a gun, even though the only weapon she'd ever fired was a .22-caliber rifle at a county fair booth some years before.

Without a watch, she judged time by the position of the sun and estimated it had been at least four hours when she caught sight of the waters of the Río Grande, sparkling in the shallow valley a quarter mile ahead of them. And not a bit too soon. For the past half hour she'd been shifting her weight in the saddle to relieve the growing numbness in her buttocks.

Helverson called a rest stop to water the horses and mules, and she dismounted with a groan, thinking with fearful anticipation that the journey had just begun. She led her roan down a sandy cutbank to the water's edge. Flood was already there, holding the long tether that roped the mules together. Her uncle and the guide were standing on a high point of ground above them, talking and pointing across the river, as if discussing their route. She was too far away to hear their words.

"The land looks so dry, I'm surprised at how much water is in this river in summer," she remarked, removing her hat and wiping a sleeve across her forehead.

"When I was in the cavalry out here, this river often meant the difference between life and death for us . . . *and* the Apaches." Flood smiled at her. "The Río Grande is the blood of this land . . . even more than the Mississippi is for the center of the country. Always a dependable source of water from the mountains. Long north-south flow. Probably the only thing that made this land habitable, even for the early Indians."

"I've read that most of the Indians built their pueblos near this river."

He nodded. "A thousand years ago, some of the pueblos were back in the remote cañons and on the high mesas. But, for some reason . . . maybe drought . . . many of them moved toward the river a couple centuries before the Spaniards came up here from Mexico." He squinted up the river. "Then the fights with the Spanish soldiers once more destroyed a few of their villages, and they were forced to move and rebuild."

"Uncle Mac says the treasure is back in one of those old cliff dwellings," she said, lowering her voice so that it could not be heard above the gurgling of the water over a shallow gravel bed.

"So he says. But there are hundreds of cliff dwellings scattered back in those cañons. Finding the right one will be the problem."

She glanced up toward the higher ground where her uncle and the guide were still conversing. "What do you think of Helverson?" she asked, trying to draw him out.

"Too soon to tell. Seems OK, but I don't know how we're going to keep him from finding out about the treasure. He'll be suspicious if your uncle fires him just when we're getting close. And if he does that, I hope we can still find the place . . . and find our way back. I don't see any practical way that we can keep the existence of the treasure a secret from him."

"Then I hope he's trustworthy. Seems as if we're taking a big chance."

"That's my feeling, too. I was trying to think of some way to disarm him when we get near the place. Besides that rifle, he carries a handgun and a knife."

"Then we'd have to take him back as a prisoner," she mused. "Besides the danger of that, he might escape, or purposely get us lost. Uncle Mac is no mountain man. And all this wild country is certainly new to me."

"My earlier time out here was spent mostly on horse patrols to the south. From the maps I've looked at, the land west of here for more than two hundred miles is nothing but deserts and buttes and sandstone cañons cut by streams that twist every which way. It's not going to be easy."

Just then McGinnis and Helverson led their horses down the bank toward the river, and Flood stopped talking. Merliss tied her horse to an upthrust piece of driftwood that was bleached bone-white, then took her canteen from the saddle horn and walked away upstream to fill it.

She took a good drink of cold water, filled the canteen, and returned with it. Then she dug into her saddlebags for the small Kodak box camera she'd purchased on a whim at Santa Fé. Cameras were becoming cheaper and simpler to operate, especially with the availability of celluloid film on rolls. It seemed people everywhere—especially travelers—were snapping photos.

She turned the knob on the side of the box until the number 1 appeared in the shaded window. Then she carefully pointed the lens downriver at Marc Flood, Uncle Mac, and Helverson. Gazing down into the viewfinder on top, she snapped the shutter. She glanced at the angle of the sun. Nearly overhead. She had taken photographs before, but not in such intense sunlight. Maybe the men's hats wouldn't shade their faces completely. She began to wind the film for another shot when suddenly something clamped her elbow. She gasped.

"You taking pictures of me?" Helverson growled, almost in her ear.

"I . . . uh . . . why, yes." Startled, she tried to back away from him. "And Uncle Mac, too." A chill went up her back at his grim expression. "Just want to make a record of our trip.

Uncle Mac . . . uh . . . Professor McGinnis likes to have everything documented when he's on an archaeological trip," she added as if further explanation was somehow necessary.

"I don't like anyone taking my picture," he continued. "Just one of my quirks, I guess." He backed away, giving a crooked grin that Merliss took for embarrassment at his sudden aggressive behavior.

He turned and walked back to his horse.

"What's the problem?" Flood asked, coming toward her and glancing at the departing guide.

"Nothing," she replied, feeling weak in the knees. She abruptly sat down on a large log of driftwood. The terror of her abduction in Nashville came back to overwhelm her. She hadn't realized how intensely that experience still haunted her.

"What'd he say to you?" Flood asked in a low voice, squinting toward Helverson who was tightening his saddle girth.

"He was upset because I took a picture of him." She held up her Kodak.

"A man who doesn't want his picture taken is a man with something to hide," Flood said. "Very likely on the dodge from the law." He was silent for a few seconds while Merliss took two deep breaths to calm herself. "Just keep that camera out of sight from now on," he said. "Or make sure you don't point it at him."

She nodded, got up, and slipped the Kodak back into her saddlebag. She still resolved to make a photographic record of their trip. Pictures might prove a valuable record of their journey, especially if they found the treasure.

She was disconcerted a moment later when she saw Flood approach Helverson and say something to him. Merliss could tell from the body posture that the guide didn't like it, but a few seconds later he nodded and went about his work while Flood strode away. She was sorry Flood felt it necessary to reprimand the guide, instead of just letting the incident slide. She didn't want to make an enemy this early in the trip.

The better part of an hour passed in relative silence while they consumed strips of dried beef and dry biscuits, washed down with water. The animals rested and grazed. Then they mounted up and started again. Now, instead of riding across country, they followed the course of the Río Grande upstream as it curved north by east.

She noticed her uncle consulting his notes as he rode along ahead of her. Finally he carefully put them away in a leather packet and stuffed it back into his saddlebag.

Her mind drifted to her abandoned teaching job. She had a very strict principal for a boss. He would be furious, then worried, when she didn't show up. When he eventually discovered she'd skipped away with her uncle on a treasure hunt, he'd fire her as completely undependable. And she might even be blacklisted from getting another teaching job. It was a sobering thought. Teaching was all she was really trained to do. How would she support herself? She didn't even want to think about actually sharing in the wealth of some treasure. Pie in the sky.

In this modern age, with the 20th Century just ahead, not many people considered twenty-six old. Yet, spinsterhood was looming larger with every passing year. It wasn't that she sought the security of marriage, and she certainly didn't lack for suitors. But the leering old men, or the New Orleans dandies, or the men who wanted her as a good-looking prize—these were the types she seemed to attract, discounting the married men who wanted her for a convenient mistress. Maybe she should get more involved in the social life of the church to meet some eligible men she would consider.

She heaved a sigh. What a strange set of circumstances had led to her being here on this wild trek. If she hadn't been concerned for her uncle, she would be back at her teaching job now, probably giving final examinations.

Broken country rolled away to their left, rising to what Flood called the Jemez Mountains. She studied the dark-timbered high country in the distance. How remote, serene, and eternal it seemed. How detached and unchanging—so different from the affairs of humans. All the struggling, grasping, warring, loving, sacrificing that made up life suddenly seemed inconsequential in these vast distances. The magnitude of the country certainly put their tiny party in perspective—human specks creeping alongside the trickle of water they called a river.

She shook her head to free herself of these sobering thoughts. Time for some company, for some distraction. She could see no reason for riding single-file, and so dropped back alongside Flood who was still leading the pack mules.

They rode another twenty-five miles and camped near a small village at the confluence of the Río Grande and the Chama River that flowed in from the west.

Flood gathered driftwood from the riverbank for a fire while Helverson unsaddled and hobbled the animals and turned them out to graze. McGinnis and Merliss combined to do the cooking for the four of them, although it was agreed they'd trade jobs later, since Flood assured them he had cooking experience. There was little cooking to be done anyway, since much of the food consisted of tinned vegetables and meats carried on the pack mule.

Merliss moved about the camp, saying little and trying to hide the fact that she was walking gingerly from the soreness and chaffing of the forty-five mile ride.

"How much farther do you think?" she ventured to her

uncle when they were sitting around the blaze, eating from tin plates.

"Can't rightly say," he replied. "The Río Grande cuts through some cañons just north of here. But we'll be moving west to follow the left bank of the Chama tomorrow. We're only a few miles east of the Continental Divide."

"Does that mean riding into a lot of steep mountains?" she asked, trying to sound nonchalant.

"No. We're already at a pretty high elevation in the Río Grande Valley. We'll be riding up a slight grade, all right, but it shouldn't be too noticeable."

"This is not like traveling to another part of Illinois or Kentucky," Helverson offered. "No roads out here. No way of knowing what we'll run into back in those cañons."

Merliss couldn't really make up her mind about this man as she watched him continue to eat, the firelight playing across his features. The scar on his bristled chin looked like an old groove on a jutting slab of granite. She wondered again about his abilities as guide. Her uncle or Flood could have brought them this far with an ordinary map.

She scooped up the last bite of her beef hash as she pondered their guide. If this Helverson was really wanted by the law, what had been his crime? Her unrestrained imagination conjured up all kinds of horrible possibilities—armed robbery, murder, rape? No telling. If they'd hired a violent criminal, what was to stop him from taking the treasure and leaving their bodies for the vultures? A tremor ran through her at the thought.

She desperately wanted a good hot soak in a bathtub. But with darkness had come the chill air off the mountains that confirmed their altitude. And the river water was even colder. The bath would have to wait.

"Good night, all," she said. "It's been a long day. I'm

going to turn in." She stood up and stretched her arms over her head. Not until she saw Helverson's eyes on her did she realize how this motion pushed her prominent breasts against the cotton blouse she wore. She dropped her arms and turned away, shivering from an inner chill that had nothing to do with the night air.

Chapter Ten

Six Miles West of Folsom, New Mexico
June 7, 1898

William Ellsworth "Elza" Lay held the reins of his horse and nervously tried to read the face of his pocket watch in the bright moonlight. Almost eleven-thirty. The westbound Colorado & Southern was due any minute, but he could see more than a mile down the track, and there was no sign of it yet.

Lay was not nervous because of his lack of experience as a train robber. Just the reverse. Members of the Wild Bunch had hit this train in the same place twice before, and Lay thought Butch Cassidy, who had planned this attempt, should have used a little more originality. Although they formed loose alliances and helped one another, the fluid, ever-changing group of outlaws that came and went from the Hole-in-the-Wall took orders from no one.

Elza Lay did not go out on a job with just anyone. And the two men waiting with him had proven they could be relied upon. Sam Ketchum, brother of Tom "Black Jack" Ketchum, was a steady veteran of numerous robberies. The other man, one of three outlaw brothers, Harvey Logan, alias Kid Curry, was hard to figure. A humorless, taciturn man, Kid Curry certainly didn't lack for brains or courage. Because of his ferocity, the newspapers had taken to calling him the "Tiger of the Wild Bunch," a name he prized almost as much as his alias, a name borrowed from another admired outlaw, Mike Curry. Lately, though, Logan had been going by the name of W. H. Frank. Lay himself had used other names to confuse identification and pursuit, one of these being William H. McQueston, which he favored when working as a ranch hand.

Even though Lay had quit handling the remuda at the WS Ranch to join Sam Ketchum and Kid Curry on this job, he was uneasy. He felt they were pressing their luck. Just a month ago he had taken part in a robbery near Wilcox, Wyoming where the take was minimal because Butch and Sundance had used entirely too much dynamite on the safe and had blown not only the safe but the express car and most of the currency into unusable pieces. Even with little to show for their efforts, the Bunch had to split up and run, with tenacious posses on their trail. One of the most determined individuals who pursued them was Pinkerton operative Charley Siringo. Fortunately he'd followed a false lead to Mississippi. By the time Siringo got straightened out, Lay and the others were safely away into the wilds of Wyoming where even the bravest lawmen hesitated to go.

Lay took a deep breath and looked up at the stars. The bright moon had dimmed his view of the spangled night sky. The moonlight was fortuitous. It enabled them to see without lanterns, and it cast black shadows, keeping their faces hidden beneath their hat brims, even without the bandannas they wore as masks. But it didn't much matter, he reflected, whether they were recognized or not; he and the others were already wanted for so many bank and train robberies, one more would make no difference.

He had seriously, and privately, considered quitting the Outlaw Trail and going straight, but two things had kept him from trying. One, he had been involved in so many robberies in several states that it would take amnesty from four or five governors. Not likely to happen. And the second reason was more compelling: he needed money. Cowboying was the only work he knew. He was good with livestock, but couldn't afford his own spread. He couldn't picture himself growing old and broken down on subsistence wages. Some of the men had facetiously suggested that Lay pull and sell some of his half dozen gold teeth when he was strapped for funds between jobs. As a man hunted by the Pinkertons, sheriffs, railroad posses, and various other law men, he had to stay on the move, or leave the country completely. No, he had gone too far down this road to think of reversing his course now.

Lay took off his hat and wiped his forehead. The June night had become very still, and he was sweating from the exertion of dragging limbs and brush to form a six-foot pile on the tracks.

A faint noise in the distance drew his attention. A speck of light was far down the track. Several seconds later, the sound of a chuffing locomotive distinguished itself.

"Light it!" Kid Curry ordered.

Ketchum moved forward and squatted by the pile of sage, creosote bush, and mesquite. A few seconds later, a tiny flame flickered. Then the brush caught and blazed up, illuminating the three men.

The train was drawing closer, and Lay mounted his horse. The engine slowed and finally came to a grinding halt several yards from the blazing pile. Engineers had earlier tried plowing through, sweeping burning brush aside with their cow-catchers. But, after two locomotives had been derailed by rocks and iron rods, the trainmen now took no chances.

Curry, gun in hand, leaped to the cab of the locomotive, and Lay heard him giving orders to the trainmen. With practiced efficiency, Ketchum was uncoupling the locomotive, tender, and express cars from the rest of the train. Then the engine began to roll forward and shoved aside the still-burning remains of the brush pile.

Lay let it go by, with Curry still holding the engineer hostage. Almost by default, Lay had the job of handling the dynamite that would blow the express car safe. The other two were deathly afraid of explosives. Lay rode up to the express car, when the train stopped a quarter mile farther along. He pounded on the side door with the heel of his boot. "Open up!"

No response.

"Open up, or I'll blast this car to hell!"

Silence.

"You've got as long as it takes me to set this dynamite and light the fuse to open the door!" Lay called, dismounting and reaching into his saddlebags. Just as he approached the door with a bundle of four wrapped sticks of dynamite and some blasting caps, he heard the lock click, and the messenger slid open the big door.

"Get down outta there, unless you want to open that safe for me," Lay said to the uniformed messenger. The moonlight glinted dully from the Wells Fargo badge on the front of his cap as he nodded silently and jumped down out of the car.

"Back over there!" Lay ordered, waggling the barrel of his pistol. Then he holstered the weapon and hitched himself up into the lighted car where a lamp burned in a wall sconce. "One last chance to open this safe," Lay suggested, hoping he wouldn't have to deal with the dynamite that was beginning to bead with sweat. He much preferred black powder, but it was bulky to carry on horseback and very susceptible to dampness. Nitroglycerin in the form of dynamite was probably better, if it could be kept cool. He took two sticks and caps and wrapped them with a strip of cloth around the handle of the iron floor safe. Twisting the fuses together, he fastened a six-foot piece of cordite to them and led it to the door. Then he jumped down, took a match from his vest pocket, and lighted the fuse. Vaulting into the saddle, he rode about fifty yards away. Several seconds later a muffled boom blew a cloud of smoke and dust from the open door.

It was neatly done. The iron door on the safe was ajar with little damage to anything else. The take appeared to be less than a thousand dollars in currency, Lay noted with disgust as he scooped it out. "Damn!" He didn't stop to count it, but merely shoved the bills into his saddlebags. "Let's go boys! Slim pickins' tonight."

Ketchum and Curry backed away, still holding guns on the trainmen. Then the three men mounted and spurred away toward the southwest.

It was just past five-thirty in the morning, and daylight was showing the folded foothills of the Sangre de Cristo Mountains, when the trio reined up near Turkey Cañon, ten miles north of Cimarron, New Mexico.

"Damned good thing the cave's only a couple miles farther," Ketchum said. "These horses are done in."

The three men sat looking toward the brightening sky in the east.

Curry leaned forward on his saddle horn. "I can hardly wait to get down and stretch. My butt's numb."

The horses' heads were hanging and they were blowing, even though they'd been proceeding at a walking gait for the last half mile.

"How much did you get out of that safe?" Ketchum asked.

Lay shook his head. "Not enough to make it worthwhile. We need to pick our targets better."

"Well, we'll divvy up when we get to the cave, and get something to eat," Curry said, touching his horse with his spurs.

"Boys, I don't think it's a good idea to go to that cave," Lay said.

Curry pulled up. "Why? That's where we always hole up. It's got a good spring in the back of it. Nobody's found us yet."

"That's just the problem," Lay said. "We've become too predictable . . . hitting the same train in the same place, hiding out in the same place. I've got a bad feeling about it this time. They'll have a posse on our tail for sure, probably riding down from Trinidad. They'll be on fresh horses, well-armed, and probably mad as hell."

"So? What's new?" Ketchum shrugged.

"I just think we need to ride on to find another hide-out. It wouldn't take an expert tracker to follow us to this cave."

"Where, then? These horses are finished," Curry said.

"We passed a ranch just south of here where we can steal some fresh ones. Let's ride into the cañon country on the other side of the Río Grande. Take maybe a day or two, but we can throw 'em off our trail. If they get too close, there are plenty of places to bushwhack 'em."

"Hell, you talk like there's a posse breathing down our necks," Ketchum growled, pushing back his hat and squinting off at the tranquil sunrise.

"There will be. You can bet on it," Lay insisted. "If you boys don't want to ride on, we'll divide up right here, and I'll go on alone."

"You must have a mighty strong feeling that it ain't safe here," Curry said, eyeing him.

"You damn' betcha I don't think it's safe here. We're really pushing our luck coming back here every time," Lay said. When the other two were silent for several seconds, he asked: "Well, what's it gonna be?" The horses seemed to be regaining their wind and were beginning to crop the nearby grass.

"OK, if you're that antsy about it, we'll all go," Curry said. "Can't hurt to find a new place. At least over in cañon country, we'll be that much closer to Hole-in-the-Wall if we have to make a break for it." He dismounted with a grunt. "I gotta take a minute and get the kinks out."

Lay, also, climbed down. "Tell you what . . . if it's agreeable, let's give the horses a little rest while we split the take, then we'll backtrack to that ranch, and help ourselves to three fresh mounts." He reached into his saddlebags.

The looted safe had given up only $276 apiece.

"Damn! Is that it?" Curry looked disgustedly at the greenbacks in his hand. "I oughta go to work for wages."

"Ain't hardly worth the risk of getting my neck stretched," Ketchum added, folding the bills and stuffing them into the side pocket of his jeans. "You sure you ain't holding out on us, Lay?" He arched his eyebrows.

Elza Lay shook his head as he held open the flap of his saddlebag. "Look for yourself, or search me if you want to. We just can't keep hitting the same express car over and over and not expect them to get wise and start varying their schedule of shipment."

"You think they'll come after us for this?" Ketchum asked.

Curry gave him a pitying look. "We held up their train and blew their safe. What do you think? Wouldn't matter if we'd got only one silver dollar. We slipped under their guard and hit 'em with an uppercut. This is a fight to the death. Those railroad people aren't gonna rest until we're all dead, or they are."

"You're right," Lay agreed. "At first, it might have been the money, but now it's the principle of the thing. We've hurt the pride of Wells Fargo and the railroad barons. Now it's just a deadly game to show who's best."

"Then let's go," Curry said, gathering up his reins and

mounting. "If there's a posse on our trail, I want to make those bastards earn their money, just like we're doing."

A few minutes later the rays of the rising sun were warming Elza Lay and the other two riders as they picked their way along the eastern foothills of the Sangre de Cristo range toward the ranch that would supply them fresh transportation into the rugged cañon country beyond the Río Grande.

Chapter Eleven

Quantus Tremor Est Futurus

"I'm sure we haven't come three leagues from the river yet," Professor Roddy McGinnis said, holding his horse on a tight rein and studying the formation of the sandstone cliffs on the opposite side of the Chama River.

"Three leagues?" Helverson almost snorted. "What kind of measurement is that? Along the course of the Chama, it's been about eight miles."

Flood, a few yards downwind of them, could hear the conversation plainly. He doubted that the fierce New Mexico sun, pouring into the narrow cañon, could completely account for the redness of Helverson's face. Flood unwrapped the end of the lead line from his saddle horn and handed it to Merliss, then kneed his horse forward. "What's the problem?" he asked.

"He won't let me see the directions he's got written down," Helverson said. "Keeps talking distances in leagues instead of miles."

"My . . . uh . . . directions indicate a stream comes in from the northwest. We follow that stream. But I'm sure we're not there yet," McGinnis said.

As he spoke, Helverson had dismounted and was holding an Army compass in his hand. Then, walking a dozen steps to his left, he stopped and appeared to be aligning the compass with some mark on the far shore. All Flood saw was a spur of sandstone that had split off from the bluff and was jutting out at a slight angle.

"Is there anything in that diary that describes specific landmarks, besides trees or rivers?" Flood asked the professor in an undertone.

"No. The directions are pretty general after we leave the Río Grande."

"Then what is he doing with that compass? Looks like he's taking sightings on some landmarks of his own," Flood observed quietly.

"By the Star of the Magi, he's supposed to be our guide," McGinnis growled.

"But unless he's been to the exact location before, how does he know where to guide us?" Flood muttered.

"These cañons look pretty much alike to me. I suppose he's got some spots marked where he takes compass bearings on certain sandstone spires so he knows exactly where he is. Like coastal piloting for a sailor."

In a louder voice Flood said: "The cliff dwelling we're looking for was once known as the Stone Castle. Do you know of such a place?"

Helverson didn't reply for a few seconds, but then snapped the compass case shut and came toward them. "No such name that I know of. Could be called anything now, depending on who named it," he said. "Every new naturalist who comes digging has some old ruin named for him...like Wetherill and Bandelier. But, from what the professor's told me, I have to go with my best guess. And I say this is the side cañon you're looking for. This cañon runs thirty or forty miles back that way and does a lot of looping around on itself. If we don't find the ruins you're looking for right off, we might be two or three weeks climbing up to them, one by one.

I take it you'll know the right place when you find it."

"I'll be able to identify it." McGinnis nodded. "But I know this is not the turn-off. We'll move on up the Chama a little farther." He said firmly: "Mount up."

Helverson shrugged. "It's your money and your time."

The party moved on up the river. Helverson indicated his disagreement with their route by dropping back and letting McGinnis take the lead. They rode another five slow miles by Flood's estimate. No one spoke as the sun grew higher and hotter in the windless cañon. The red and yellow sandstone walls finally pinched off the south side riverbank where they were riding, and they were forced to find a shallow ford where they could cross on a sandbar. The deepest part of the river barely reached their stirrups. The bottom was all firm gravel and small rocks, much to the relief of Flood who was leading the pack mules. The mules apparently sensed the treacherous quicksand that was plentiful along these streams and balked at entering the water.

Another mile of riding along the opposite bank brought them to the confluence of another unnamed stream. They halted for another conference. McGinnis dismounted and walked off by himself to consult his notes again. After a few minutes he returned and conferred with Helverson who was plainly not in agreement. But McGinnis was adamant, and they branched off up the side cañon, necessarily proceeding at a slower pace along the narrowing gorge of red sandstone. The bare walls on both sides of them varied in height from one to two-hundred feet above their heads.

Hour after hour their horses plodded along, following the sinuous stream. White, fluffy summer clouds drifted overhead in the deep blue sky. Flood noticed Helverson scrutinizing the sky and the cliff tops. At first he thought the guide was trying to orient himself, but gradually came to realize the big man was studying the weather. Being caught in a summer flash flood in this cañon could very well prove fatal. Because of the twisting course of the silt-laden stream, they were forced to cross and re-cross, and sometimes wade up against the foot-deep current. As Helverson's horse splashed out of the water, it stepped into some sandy muck, then snorted and jerked back in alarm as its front feet began to sink. The guide jabbed him with his spurs, and the horse yanked its feet free and lunged back into the stream. Helverson dismounted and, breaking off a thick willow, began to lead the animal, probing the bottom ahead of him for quicksand with the stick.

By late afternoon they paused, drenched in sweat, on a high sandbar covered with willows and ferns. Everyone dismounted.

"We need to find some fresh water," the professor said, shaking his nearly empty canteen. "The stuff in this river isn't fit to drink."

"Tie off the horses and everybody have a look around," Helverson directed. "There're usually some fresh water springs in these cañons, if there's been a good snow melt in the mountains."

They split up, and a few minutes later Merliss discovered a small stream of fresh, cold water flowing from a willow-covered sand bank. They all gathered, drinking and then filling their canteens. They rested briefly while the animals drank from the stream and browsed on the tender willow leaves.

As they moved on, the cañon broadened out to a hundred yards or more, and their route became higher and drier. To save the horses, they all dismounted and walked, leading their mounts.

They camped in late afternoon on a higher bank away from the river. Flood had also been watching the sky and felt they probably would have no rain this night. The campsite Helverson had selected was relatively safe, since it was at least fifty vertical feet from the bottom of the cañon on a benchland of dirt and gravel.

Firewood wasn't plentiful, but they managed to gather enough dead brush from some former high-water mark to cook some bacon and ward off the after-dark chill.

Flood had helped Helverson unpack the mule and picket the animals. Flood carefully positioned his bedroll between Helverson and Merliss. He was not expecting any overt move from the guide, but was taking no chances.

Two days later, Flood was finally becoming toughened to the trail. He had not thought to bring a razor, nor had McGinnis, so the two men were sporting several days of stubble, the professor's white whiskers contrasting with his wind-burned face. Helverson, on the other hand, had kept himself shaven and as clean as if he were sitting in the shade on the plaza at Santa Fé. Apparently Helverson, as a professional guide, knew the tricks of wilderness travel.

The next morning they came in sight of their first cliff dwelling, a cluster of stone structures about a hundred and fifty feet above the valley floor. When they got closer, they tied off the horses and mules in the thick willows along the small river in the bottom and then went searching for a way up to the ancient dwellings. Whatever path the vanished Indians had used was long since washed away, and they searched in vain for footholds and handholds cut into the sandstone. "Maybe used notched logs for ladders that they could pull up after them," Flood commented.

"Not likely, unless they had a series of terraces that have washed out since they were here," McGinnis answered.

"I think we can make it up from here!" Helverson yelled as

he emerged over the top of the foliage about eighty yards away.

Where frost and water and plants had forced their way into cracks in the cliff face, sand and slabs of rock had been broken loose over the centuries and fallen to form a rough path that angled up toward the corner of the cave. With Helverson leading, they struggled upward, slipping and sliding in the loose shale. Merliss skinned her shin, and Flood took her hand and pulled her in the roughest spots where they were forced to climb over huge, jagged boulders.

Flood made sure Helverson was leading, and that his own Colt was loaded and ready on his hip. If this proved to be the cave with the treasure, he wanted to be ready for whatever might come, including Helverson's reaction. He still instinctively distrusted the big guide.

They finally gained the lower corner of the cave opening and discovered the ancient ones had constructed a stone retaining wall in front of the cave lip and filled rock and dirt in behind it to form a flat, stable extension of the cave floor. The wall was about eight feet high, and they took turns boosting and pulling each other up to the top of this wall.

Helverson was on top first, lying flat on his stomach and reaching down to give McGinnis a hand up, while Merliss and Flood waited their turns below. The wiry professor was nearly to the top when suddenly his grip on Helverson's big hand came loose. *"Aaagghh!"* His body came hurtling back down and slammed into Merliss.

Flood reacted in a flash and lunged for both of them as they slid in a tangle toward a thirty-foot vertical drop. He grabbed one of them in each hand and felt clothing rip as their momentum dragged him toward the edge as well. He threw his legs out and dug in his heels. The three of them slid to a stop at the lip of the drop-off, powdery red dust billowing up to choke them. The only thing, besides Flood's quick grab, that had saved McGinnis and his niece from going over the edge to the sharp rocks below was several stunted bushes that had taken root in the thin soil. In the few seconds of silence that followed, Merliss coughed.

"Don't make any sudden moves," Flood cautioned. "Stay very still until I can work my way back up there." He let go of them and carefully turned around. Then, using his fingers and toes to get what grip he could, clawed his way back up to the narrow ledge from which they'd fallen. When he reached it, he glanced upward and saw Helverson, gazing down at them intently from the top of the retaining wall. "Left our climbing rope on the pack mule," he said.

"Helluva time to think of it," Flood muttered, pulling off his belt. Then he lay down on his stomach and let down a loop formed by the buckle. After several misses, he finally managed to drop the loop over one of Merliss's booted ankles. He jiggled the loop tight and slowly dragged her upward until she could twist around to grab his hand. When she was safely beside him, he again let down the belt as far as he could, and McGinnis got hold of it. Flood pulled until he could reach the professor's hand and inched the lean man upward until all three were on the ledge.

"Let me go back down to the mules for the rope before we try this again," Flood said. "Better yet, you go get it, Professor. I'll keep an eye on things here. You're agile enough to climb over that trail . . . better than I am," he added for Helverson's benefit.

McGinnis, hatless, slapped the dust from his coat and looked at Flood, then at Helverson. "By the Rock of Gibraltar, that was close! What the hell happened, Helverson?" The professor's oath seemed to lack its usual explosive force.

"My hand was sweaty," the guide replied matter-of-factly,

wiping his palms on his pants legs.

No apologies in word or manner for nearly causing the deaths of two of the party, Flood thought to himself. He took a close look at Helverson. The man would have been a good poker player. Flood could not read any expression at all. But he kept an eye on the guide who went over to sit on a wall and roll himself a cigarette.

When the professor returned with the coil of rope over his shoulder, Flood said: "All right. There will be no more climbing until at least one is secured, and we're all roped together."

"If one falls, we all fall. Is that it?" Helverson smirked, grinding out his smoke.

"Damned sight safer than the way we were just trying to do it," Flood snapped.

McGinnis had tossed down the rope and was already poking through the empty rooms.

Flood took Merliss's hand, and the two of them went exploring. There were at least twenty rooms, counting those on the second floor toward the higher front of the cave. Many of them were adjoining. Nothing was left but dust. Here and there were a few small, shriveled corn cobs.

"What's this?" Merliss asked, handing Flood a tiny article she'd picked up from the dusty floor.

"Looks like a turkey bone needle," Flood said, turning over the smooth sliver.

She looked at him. "There's no treasure here," she whispered, glancing around. "We've looked in every room."

"If there really is treasure, I doubt it's going to be lying around in plain sight," Flood said. "But if we're going to search every one of these old cliff dwellings up and down these cañons, it might take us the rest of the summer. I guess I thought your uncle would be able to go right to it."

132

"Apparently the directions in Peter Stirling's diary aren't all that specific."

"I know he's the expert, and I probably couldn't make anything of it, but I wish he'd read his notes to us."

"I'm still nervous about Helverson," she whispered, her words sounding hollow in the small bare room where they stood.

"Me, too," Flood nodded. "How are you feeling?" he asked to change the subject.

"Bruised," she answered. "Uncle Mac isn't all that heavy, but he fell on me with nothing but elbows and hip bones." She grinned over her shoulder at him as she ducked her head and led the way back out the low, T-shaped doorway.

McGinnis was securing the rope to a boulder and preparing to let himself down into a circular kiva, a rock-lined, roofless room that was sunken in the cave floor.

Flood and Merliss walked to the retaining wall and sat where they could watch and keep an eye on Helverson who was standing at the far end of the cave and staring off downcañon.

"Marc, it's a lucky thing you and Uncle Mac met," Merliss said thoughtfully. "He could never have made this trip alone, or even with just me. He really needed a good, strong man he could trust." She glanced at the guide who stood with his back to them, one foot on the retaining wall about forty yards away.

Flood shrugged. "I think it was probably meant to be. I don't really believe in luck."

"I didn't even thank you for saving our lives a few minutes ago," she said.

"Reflex action. Luck. The bushes were there, or I couldn't have held onto you."

"I thought you just said you didn't believe in luck," she chided him.

"Only an expression," he smiled.

"Marcus Flood, what's your real name . . . Don Quixote of la Mancha, the redresser of injuries, the righter of wrongs, the protector of damsels, the terror of giants, and the winner of battles?"

"Not quite, but I'm working on it, especially that part about being the terror of giants."

They sat for several long seconds, letting the heavy silence envelop them.

Finally she said quietly: "I'm beginning to have a bad feeling about all this."

"We're just in a strange place," Flood said, feeling a need somehow to reassure her. "We're sitting where humans last lived and walked more than six hundred years ago. It's a little eerie. But nothing to really fear, unless you believe in ghosts."

"It's not that. I find these old stone rooms fascinating. I like history. I don't know. . . ." She shook her head slowly. "It's just a feeling. Maybe a woman's intuition."

"Him?" Flood inquired, trying to put a face on her fears by nodding slightly toward Helverson.

"He's part of it, I guess. I can't really define it."

"Your uncle is so sure of finding this treasure, what do you think it will do to him if he comes up empty?"

"It wouldn't crush him, if that's what you're asking. He'd be disappointed, of course," she replied thoughtfully, as if trying to visualize such a situation. "In his line of work there are lots of disappointments. But he's really fired up about this . . . more than I've ever seen him about anything before. I think he'd turn over every rock in New Mexico before he'd give up."

"That might take him a while. You know, even if this treasure *was* actually hidden here somewhere in the Fifteen Hundreds, what are the chances it hasn't been discovered or moved by now?"

"If that's a question, you're asking the wrong person," she said. "All those ruins in Chaco Cañon back there a few miles were first excavated two years ago. And several of these other, larger ruins. And nothing was found but some artifacts."

"And the Mesa Verde ruin and the ones Bandelier dug through," Flood added. "Even if there is treasure in one of these, it probably won't be too many years before archaeologists find it. Since the Indian threat is about gone, every one of these little, obscure stone cliff villages will be looted by thieves or professionals."

"Regardless of any treasure," she said, "the mysteries of these unknown peoples are being discovered a little at a time. Pretty soon everything about them may be revealed. And the world will be the poorer for it. The world needs a few unexplained mysteries."

Just then they heard McGinnis's muffled voice. "Hey, give me a hand up out of here!"

They went to help pull him out of the kiva.

"Find anything?" Flood asked, pulling on the rope as the professor held on and walked up the side of the stone pit.

"Nope. Didn't figure I would." He was covered from head to foot in dust. Rivulets of sweat coursed down his face into his white stubble. He'd recovered his hat, and it was thrust onto his head, bent into an odd shape. "Just the caved-in roof." He pulled up the loose rope and began coiling it around his elbow and shoulder. "Didn't think we were on the right track here, but had to check it out to make sure." He turned away. "Helverson!" he yelled. "Let's try for that one you said is about five miles on up this cañon. We've got enough daylight. We'll camp there."

★ ★ ★ ★ ★

When they arrived about mid-afternoon, they found the next ruin to be only slightly larger. This one was on the opposite side of the cañon and faced southwest, so the afternoon sun shone into the cave, giving the yellowish sandstone structures a warm glow and illuminating the jumble of rooms.

After watering the animals, the men moved them back from the danger of the quicksand flats along the stream, loosened the cinches, and slipped the bits from their mouths to allow them to graze on whatever vegetation they could reach.

In addition to throwing the coil of rope over his shoulder, Helverson slid his rifle from its scabbard as they began to search for a way up to the mouth of the cave. "Saw a rattler back there," the guide said when Flood questioned the rifle. "They're likely all through these rocks. Just want to be prepared. If you can hit one of those slithering devils with a pistol, you're a lot better shot than I am." He smiled grimly.

Again the party split up to look for a way up since there was no obvious path to the cave a hundred or more feet above their heads. Flood made sure he was behind Helverson while McGinnis and Merliss plowed through the heavy growth of brush and up the piles of detritus that lay along the base of the cliff. This time, they found footholds cut into a natural split in the sandstone. Flood called to the others, and, with Helverson leading, they were soon ascending the rough stairs. Six feet from the lip of the cave floor, the steps were washed out or worn away. Flood hunted around and found four rocks large enough to stack for steps. They boosted and pulled each other to the top, then began the search once more. Except for a round watchtower at one corner that commanded a view upcañon, this complex of dwellings contained probably fifteen more rooms than the previous one. But this pueblo was just as vacant as the previous ruin had been.

Broken shards of pottery lay here and there, covered with the dust of centuries, and Flood noticed the ceiling of the high cave blackened in places from hundreds of ancient fires.

McGinnis went directly to one of two roofless kivas, the circular, rock-lined pits. Flood thought the old man must have some indication that the treasure was stored in one of these. The kiva roof of mud-plastered saplings had collapsed into the bottom, and the old man went to poking about in the débris with the walking stick he carried with him.

Keeping a wary eye on Helverson, who seemed to take no interest in their wanderings, Flood and Merliss went exploring again. Either the ancient Indians had taken everything of value with them when they moved out hundreds of years before, or pot hunters and looters had cleaned out anything left behind. Here and there were small pieces of woven cloth that had been preserved in the dry atmosphere. On the back wall of the cave were some well-preserved red and white paintings of stick figures that appeared to depict hunters pursuing deer.

They stepped from one room to another, the bright sunshine splashing the mud-plastered walls with a yellow glow through the window and doorway openings. They found themselves talking in whispers, as if normal voices might disturb the heavy silence that permeated the place.

After a quick tour of the rooms, Flood and Merliss came back out to bask in the sunshine bathing the cave. Flood sat down on the ground and stared off into the heat haze of the cañon below them. A hawk soared on the thermal updrafts in the distance. Probably scouring the brush far below for a rodent of some kind, Flood guessed.

He looked at the woman beside him. What was she thinking? The westering sun shone on the deep, blue-green eyes, and he could hardly pull his gaze away. He had managed to keep his eyes and mind on business while they rode and climbed and explored, but now she sat next to him, a dust-covered gem, her thick black hair pulled back and tied at the nape of her neck. She appeared tired and worn down, but no amount of dirt or fatigue could mar her basic beauty. He took a deep breath and concentrated on retying the lace of his short boot.

A rifle shot blasted the stillness. While the echoes were still slamming back and forth from the cañon walls, Flood sprang to his feet, thumbing the leather thong off his pistol.

"By the hammer of Thor! You almost shot my head off, you crazy bastard!" McGinnis screamed.

Flood raced around the corner of a stone wall, gun drawn. Helverson stood there, holding his Winchester. McGinnis was just peering over the lip of the sunken kiva, his face gone pale under his sunburn.

"Sorry," Helverson said in a flat voice. "I was taking a shot at a snake down there. You just poked your head up at the wrong second."

"Like hell!" McGinnis was visibly shaken.

They all stood staring at each other for several seconds. Nobody spoke. Then the professor threw a knee up, and Flood helped him climb out of the kiva.

"Working around you is more dangerous than being the king's official food taster," McGinnis grunted, glaring at Helverson.

"Where was the snake?" Flood asked.

"Big rattlesnake just crawling out of that last room down there." The guide pointed. "I missed him. Went down the slope into the brush."

Merliss looked curiously at Flood. He turned away with her and muttered: "There were no marks in the dust to indicate any snakes had been in that room. No bird tracks, no kangaroo rat droppings. Nothing. The dust in that room hadn't been disturbed for years until we went through there a few minutes ago."

Her blue eyes were now wide with fear as the four of them started back down the rock staircase toward their horses.

Chapter Twelve

At the Cave

Dan Helverson had been studying the sky for the past hour and suddenly made his decision. "We'll go into camp about a mile up ahead," he said to McGinnis who was riding nearby.

"We've got at least three more hours of daylight," the professor objected.

"There's a big cave for shelter. It's getting ready to storm," Helverson replied evenly, not wanting to aggravate the old man further. "We've been lucky these summer thunderstorms have held off so far."

Above the cañon walls the billowing white clouds were massing and forming dark bases. He estimated they'd have nothing to worry about until sometime after dark. Even though the clouds were boiling up into thunderheads thousands of feet high, he could feel no hint of breeze on his face in this deep cañon where all movement of air was cut off at the moment.

The cave materialized right where Helverson knew it to be. The animals splashed across the foot-deep stream, and they rode up the sloping sand bank under the cool rock overhang. The mouth of the cave was at least seventy feet high and a hundred and twenty feet wide, formed by the current sweeping for centuries about the bend and undercutting the red sandstone.

Merliss and Flood gathered enough driftwood for a good fire while McGinnis unpacked the cooking gear and tin plates. Helverson took his turn as cook, creating a stew of canned tomatoes, dried onions, and a rabbit he'd shot about two hours before. Biscuits left over from breakfast completed the bill of fare.

He kept to himself, trying to act as natural as possible, but knew Flood was watching him closely. There was little talking during the meal. Helverson attributed it to the long days and many miles. They were all trail weary from riding and climbing up and down the rocks. The first flush of excitement had worn off, and the trip had become one of slogging endurance.

As Helverson leaned back on his saddle and spooned up the stew, he kept his eyes on his plate. He had the uneasy feeling the girl could read his thoughts if he looked directly at her. Merliss was certainly an attractive woman, and he dared not let her nearness become a source of distraction for him.

He was disgusted with his own ineptitude. His two attempts at eliminating Roddy McGinnis had failed. And now he had aroused the suspicions of that damned bodyguard, Marc Flood. He had seen Flood and the girl talking together about him. How could he have missed McGinnis? If the old man hadn't been so spastic and jerked his head an instant before Helverson fired, the professor would now be eliminated, and Helverson would be consoling the girl over the terrible accident that had taken her uncle.

From here on he would have to be extra careful since Flood and Merliss were obviously suspicious of him. Neither of them was a fool. But they had no proof. He could catch all three of them off guard and gun them down easily enough, probably as they slept. But how could he explain their disappearance? Many people had seen them preparing for the trip.

If he returned to Santa Fé, he'd have to make up some story about their being drowned or falling from a cliff, or being swept away in a flash flood, then concoct some story to account for his own escape. Easily done, unless their bodies were ever found with bullet holes in the skulls. On the other hand, he didn't have to return to Santa Fé at all. He could turn the pack animals loose and ride on west into Arizona, then disappear entirely. But he'd have to report to D'Arcy on what had happened and why he'd failed to find the treasure. And then, loose ends always seemed to come back to trip up a man planning the perfect crime. Some unaccounted detail, some unexpected witness, a body dragged out by wolves and found by some prospector—there was always something unforeseen. D'Arcy had wanted the deaths, first of all, to appear accidental. So far, he'd been frustrated in that.

He collected the tin plates and utensils and took them to the stream where he proceeded to scour them clean with sand and water. He had to formulate a plan of action. He dared not fail in his assignment. The whole order of the Western Templars was depending on him. As he squatted at the edge of the stream, he reflected that deviousness was not his style. He was no actor who could convincingly pretend to be someone he was not. But he'd been forced into that rôle. The old man was gullible enough, but the bodyguard and the girl had been leery of him from the beginning. He remembered how he'd said as little as possible, hoping to project the persona of a taciturn mountain man who knew the wilderness and was strong and capable enough to lead them where they wanted to go. It was apparent McGinnis was looking for the gold in one of these cliff dwellings. If they continued to explore every ruin as they proceeded upstream, it could take weeks. Helverson knew this country. If he killed the old man and took his notes, he could probably go directly to the place where the treasure was supposed to be. But what if the notes were in shorthand or the professor had memorized the map, and not written it down? *Whatever you do, don't make the mistake of killing him before you know where the treasure is hidden,* D'Arcy had cautioned him. *Otherwise, we're no better off than the Templars who let Peter Stirling die.*

He finished cleaning the plates and utensils and stacked them beside him. He stood and stared down the cañon in the direction from which they'd just come. They had not seen another human in many days. They were isolated by miles of wilderness. He was safe enough when the time came to kill them all. "Accidents" had not worked, and his straightforward nature was impatient at continuing this farce. He regretted having to eliminate them all, especially the girl, but he could see no other choice. On the other hand, if there was no treasure to be found, then he could just finish the trip as a guide, take his pay, and go. The best plan now would be to wait. If they found the treasure, he'd catch them off guard while they were celebrating, and shoot them. He could extract the treasure and bury the bodies in one of the kivas. By stripping off and burning their clothes he could disguise the fact they were whites. If their bones were ever found, they might be mistaken for ancient Indians.

Then he'd load the pack animals with the treasure and try to figure out a secure place to put it until he could get some help in transporting it safely back to the Templar leaders. No simple task. He was sure McGinnis had brought the extra pack mules for the purpose of hauling the treasure. The old man was nearly as poor an actor as he was, pretending to be searching for a ruin that had been discovered by a dead colleague.

To move the vast treasure he could surely use the help of the two Templars in Santa Fé. He should have insisted on bringing them along, but that would have aroused even more suspicion.

He was tempted to get rid of McGinnis and Flood somehow and save the woman for himself. He rationalized that she was only an innocent bystander while the other two were the enemies of the Templars, and therefore the enemies of God. They had to be considered infidels who must be destroyed in this holy war. But, if he were to kill them outright, Merliss would hate him. And he would not take her as a captive or a slave. She seemed like someone he would consider courting, maybe even marrying. He was past due to marry, to have a family. But he was a Knight Templar. What of his devotion to duty? He was torn between duty and desire. He simply could not look upon this woman as an enemy to be eliminated. He knew he was weak. He compared himself to some of the early Templar crusaders who'd fallen prey to lust with camp followers and Saracen women, knights who'd started out with the highest ideals of sacrifice and duty and had ended up throwing over their lofty aims for lives of pleasure. They wound up living in the silks of eastern fashion, keeping harems, fallen to the level of the heathen enemy they'd come to fight.

It could not happen to him. He steeled his resolve to put duty first, regardless. There were plenty of other women in the world. He could have his choice later. First he must take care of business.

He began to formulate a plan. He would work hard and do all he could to allay their suspicions. He would allow McGinnis to lead him to the treasure. Maybe he'd wait until the professor and Flood loaded the treasure onto the pack mules. It would save him a lot of work. No! Laziness could not figure into this. He had to pick the precise moment to assure success. Flood was well-armed, and the girl also carried a small pistol. Even though he assumed both knew how to use their weapons, Helverson would have surprise on his side. Shooting them in their sleep he considered the act of a coward. Yet he knew that no human alive could resist gawking at the golden hoard as soon as it was uncovered. He would be ready to strike at the moment their attention was diverted.

The late afternoon sun on the red cañon walls dimmed as a solid mass of clouds covered the slice of overhead sky. He collected the dishes and started back to the cave, gritting his teeth as one of his periodic headaches began to come on. There was a bottle of mescal in his saddlebags that always helped alleviate the pain.

Chapter Thirteen

In the Darkness

It was the first night they had spent under roof since leaving Santa Fé, and Flood was enjoying it immensely. He'd gone to sleep rolled in his blankets on the soft sand to the soothing sounds of the stream burbling softly a few yards away. But, sometime before daylight, he was jarred out of a deep sleep by a thunderous cannonade. Groggy, he rolled over and pushed up on one elbow. Several seconds later the huge cave opening was outlined by a flash of lightning, quickly followed by blackness and an earth-shaking boom that reverberated from the cañon walls. When the noise ceased, he could hear rain sluicing down outside. He lay back with the comforting feeling of being protected from the elements in this dry cave. He heard the animals moving about nervously where they were hobbled near the rear of the cave.

"Marc, are you awake?" came Merliss's voice from the darkness.

"Yes." He could hear her moving toward him.

"Scary," she whispered as she sat down beside him, a blanket wrapped around her shoulders.

"If it wasn't so loud, it would make for good sleeping," he replied. "Almost as good as rain on a tin roof."

They sat in silence for several minutes, watching the fitful lightning display and then being engulfed by the tremendous, booming thunder. Flood pulled his watch from his boot sitting nearby. The next flash showed the time to be five-fifteen. He absently wound the watch and put it back into his boot.

"Wish I had some coffee," she whispered.

"It's about time to get up, anyway," he said. "I'll stir up the fire and put the pot on."

He pulled on his boots and fumbled his way to the dry driftwood that Helverson insisted they collect before dark, and got a small fire going from the remains of the coals in the sand. Then he set the metal spider over the flames and filled the pot with water from his canteen. Only then did he notice the figure of Helverson, standing near the cave entrance, looking out. A slight chill went over Flood. The big guide was a spectral figure in the gloom of the cave, definitely an eccentric, if not downright ominous. *Maybe,* he thought, *men who lived solitary lives in the wilderness tended to get that way, unused to the niceties of social living.* Some monks even got that way— usually men who were not really suited to the contemplative life. Yet, there was still something different about this man, he realized, as he set the coffee on to boil. Merliss had felt it, too, and had expressed it to him. And what of the two "accidents?" Yet accidents did happen. He couldn't say for sure they were anything more. And McGinnis had struck him as one of those people who was naturally accident-prone.

Daylight was creeping up through the heavy rain as he and Merliss drank their coffee, and she put some bacon in the skillet to fry.

A rumpled, puffy-eyed McGinnis was rolling out of his blankets, stretching and yawning. "Getting a little weather," he muttered.

Flood handed him a cup of coffee.

Suddenly Helverson appeared by the fire. "Time to get moving," he said.

147

"Have some breakfast," Flood offered.

"No time. This cave will be flooded within a half hour. The river's rising fast."

Flood looked again. In the gray light, a waterfall was pouring from above the cave entrance, cascading down and down, finally dissipating into a feathery veil before reaching the ground. Run-off was descending in sheets everywhere. He could see another high waterfall spilling down the opposite cañon wall. With no soil to absorb it, the rain gushed off the bare rocks, filling the river to a raging torrent.

They needed no further urging. It was obvious the water was lapping several inches higher toward the cave every minute.

"Just tie the *aparejos* to the packsaddles with a short rope," Helverson said. "We have to get across the river to higher ground. Let the mules drag the packs alongside."

Their gear and provisions were thus divided into three light loads and distributed among all three mules.

"Everything will be soaked!" McGinnis complained.

"The packs will be soaked anyway!" Helverson snapped. "The mules might have to swim. If one of them can't make it, cut the pack loose and maybe we can save one or the other."

Only then did Flood realize the seriousness of their situation. The reddish-brown current roared past the cave entrance at ten or twelve miles an hour, making it necessary for them to shout to be heard above the falling water and the rushing stream. Small trees that had been ripped up were being carried along, and uprooted willows were swirling in the foam-flecked eddies. Flood shut his mind to the thought of small boulders rolling and grinding along the bottom.

"Everybody ready?" Helverson asked, flinging the remnants of the coffee into the fire. He shoved the pot into a pack. "I'll lead. Professor, you come next, and then Merliss.

Flood, you bring up the rear with the mules, but hold them on three separate tethers. If one goes, we don't want them all to go."

"That'll be one helluva tangle with those packs floating free or tripping the mules," Flood replied.

"How much experience have you had at this?" Helverson grated.

"None."

"Then shut up and do as you're told," he snapped. "The leather packs might float briefly, but mostly they'll just drag alongside on short lines. Be sure the lines are short enough to be free of their legs. It'll work. Follow me."

Flood thought it was a stupid idea, but they didn't have time to secure the *aparejos* properly to the mules' backs anyway.

The guide mounted and urged his reluctant animal down into the water. "We may be able to wade over," he yelled over his shoulder. "If you feel your horse lose his footing, slide off and hang onto the saddle horn or the tail." He urged his bay into the rushing torrent.

Helverson was nearly to the far bank by the time Flood led the mules into the water, with the awkward packs dragging alongside. The depth of the water reached the backs of the horse, and suddenly his horse lost its footing and began to swim. It was enough to put the animal at the mercy of the current, and he was swept swiftly downstream, putting a drag on the lead ropes. This, in turn, pulled the mules' heads downstream, and they began to flounder. Yanking his knife from his boot lining, Flood slid out of the saddle and slashed frantically at the rope holding the nearest pack. He had to lunge to reach the second pack and was hacking at the line when the two mules got their footing and surged past him toward the bank. His mount also found the bottom and staggered.

Flood's wet hand slipped off the saddle horn. He made a grab for the tail and missed, feeling the force of the current carrying him downstream.

He shoved the knife beneath his belt, then struck off in a sidestroke to save himself. He'd done all he could for the packs and the animals. Everything became a watery blur as he tried to keep his head up and breathe. He bumped a mule and made a grab for the upthrust cross piece of the packsaddle. On the second try he managed to snag it. The mule now had its footing and dragged them both into shallow water and up onto the sandy bank. Flood dropped to his knees, gasping and coughing up dirty water, feeling it gush out of his nose.

He'd landed a good hundred yards downstream from the cave. The brush on the high sandbar in the bend prevented him from seeing the others. He got to his feet and staggered back toward them. A few minutes later he found them all safe. Merliss came running toward him. "Are you all right?"

"Swallowed about half the river, but I'm fine," he rasped, still spitting, feeling the grit in his mouth. He could see the two men pulling the horses and mules up away from the wide, raging stream.

"Any packs lost?" Flood asked.

"There's the last one!" McGinnis cried, sprinting like a youngster toward the half-submerged leather *aparejo* sliding along near the bank. He splashed in and grabbed it with both hands and began dragging it out of the water. He'd taken only two or three steps, when his boots began to sink into the yielding sand. "Here! Take the pack!" he yelled at Helverson. Before anyone could reach the pack, McGinnis was up to his knees in the muck. "By the LaBrea Tar Pits, I'm stuck!" he yelled, sounding more irritated than alarmed. "Give me a hand!"

Helverson was suddenly busy with the horses and didn't

appear to hear the professor. Flood and Merliss ran to the professor's aid.

"Careful! Don't get too close!" McGinnis cried.

They halted, and Flood quickly hacked off a large willow with his knife and held it out to him. The thin man leaned forward as far as he could and grasped it. They both pulled, but to no avail. He was sinking deeper. Merliss had taken a few steps closer and kept her feet moving quickly to avoid the same trap. She waded into the river and approached her uncle from the shallow water. "Here, I'm not sinking," she said to Flood. "Come this way."

Flood grabbed a short shovel from the pack on the ground and circled around behind the old man. Between the two of them they dug, quickly and frantically. Merliss threw up mud and sand with her hands like a crazed badger. This was not what Flood always imagined quicksand to be. It was yielding, all right, but not mushy. Once the body's weight had imbedded the legs, sand and water closed back in around to grip like heavy, wet cement.

McGinnis strained as they dug furiously. Finally, after several minutes, Flood got hold of one foot. By leaning forward, McGinnis twisted and wiggled his foot free. Then his other leg came slurping out of the clinging, muddy sand.

Helverson stood watching them as they crawled to solid ground, Flood holding one of the professor's short boots that had been sucked off with the laces still tied.

"Wouldn't have hurt you to help us!" Merliss spat at him, vainly wiping at the mire that coated her from the shoulders down.

"Looked like you were doing OK without me," he responded. "Besides," he said, dragging one of the packs toward him and pouring the water from it, "I'm the heaviest of all four of us. If I'd gotten mired down, it would've taken two of these mules to drag me out. And, even then, they might've pulled me in half."

He grinned at them, and Flood thought the obviously forced amusement was the most bizarre thing he'd ever seen on the guide's face. It was the first time Helverson had ever shown them a trace of a smile or grin, a heavy-handed attempt at making light of the situation. Flood turned away, wondering.

Chapter Fourteen

Into the Light

"I'm going to see if I can scout a trail up to that rimrock," Helverson said early that afternoon, when the party halted briefly to rest the animals. They had all dismounted and were standing in the hot sun. The dried mud on Flood's clothing was beginning to chafe him in half a dozen spots.

"Why?" Flood glanced at him, trying to keep the suspicion out of his voice.

"This cañon gets even narrower up ahead," he replied. "These summer thunderstorms are settling into a pattern. We came near to losing a couple of our animals and packs this morning. If there's a way to get up and travel on higher ground, we have to do it."

Flood wondered how they would reach any cliff dwellings from above, but didn't voice the question. "I'll go with you," he said quickly.

"Me, too," Merliss added.

"Suit yourselves, but I'm not waiting if you can't keep up." Helverson frowned, obviously not taken with the idea of having company. "Somebody has to stay with the mules."

"I've already strained my share of muscles for the day," McGinnis groaned, flexing his shoulders. "You go ahead. I'll rest here."

Helverson pulled his horse's head around and started

away without another word. Flood and Merliss followed. The guide retraced their trail along the stream, scanning the seamed and cracked sandstone walls on either side. They'd gone about a mile before pulling up. Flood saw no sign of a break in the wall, at least not one that horses could ascend.

Helverson dismounted and tied his mount to a bush. Then he started up the slope toward the base of the wall. Flood nodded to Merliss, and they climbed down and followed.

"A horse would have to be half mountain goat to get up here," Flood panted as his ankle-high boots slid in the shale. He turned and reached for Merliss's hand to pull her up. They were fifty feet above the cañon floor and just reaching the vertical base of the red sandstone wall. Flood looked up at Helverson's broad back as the guide toiled on ahead into a crevice in the rock.

"Where's he going?" Merliss asked in a low voice as she grabbed a small shrub to steady herself.

Flood shrugged and shook his head.

Helverson paused, apparently searching for a way to negotiate the rock face. He backed down a few steps, then approached at another angle, placing his feet carefully. Still, he slipped and slid. Where all the loose stones had been washed away, what passed for a trail was so steep, it was almost like climbing stairs up the serrated rock. Three times the passage seemed to disappear in the vertical wall, but the guide managed each time to find a crack wide enough for a man or a thin horse, but definitely not a mule with a pack.

Flood would have sworn they'd have to retrace their steps to the cañon floor, but Helverson's eyes were attuned to the eroded passage that reached all the way up the cañon wall. Where the water of a thousand years of storms had found its way to the bottom, the guide now retraced its course to the top. Flood wished he'd thought to bring the coil of rope he carried on his saddle horn. But it would be too much trouble now to go back after it. And he didn't want to lose sight of Helverson, who hadn't once looked back.

When Flood finally struggled the last few feet to the top, he reached back to give Merliss a hand up. He turned and saw the guide already eighty yards away, working his way along the smooth, rounded sandstone that comprised the barren rimrock.

"Think you want to take up mountain climbing as a sport?" He grinned at her and was immediately sorry he'd spoken when he saw her white face and the raw scrape on her right cheek. She didn't reply as she got to her feet, brushing vainly at the dried mud on her sleeves.

They started after the guide, staying safely back from the sloping rim where wind and water had rounded off the soft sandstone. They walked hand in hand, the silence comfortable between them. The view was unobstructed for miles. The plateau was mostly bare rock, humped and ridged and eroded in all directions. A feeling of freedom, almost elation came over him. They had been following the winding cañons for so many days, that he suddenly felt unrestrained. The vast country had opened up for him now that he was up above the cracks in the earth where they'd been crawling along like ants. There was something about broad vistas that had a calming effect on him. He'd become aware of this the first time he'd traveled west across the great plains and wide cañon country several years before. Woods and lakes had a beauty all their own, but there was something about wide open spaces that touched his soul.

"Where's he going?" Merliss asked.

"Don't know." Flood shrugged, almost annoyed at being interrupted from his pondering of earth and sky. He pulled his attention back to her. "Seems like he'd stand a better chance of finding a horse trail from down below than up here." He paused. The landscape he'd been admiring would be brutal to horses or mules. "Even if we got them up here, there's no shelter, nothing for them to eat, and only a few pockets of water in some of these natural tanks in the rocks." As he spoke, his gaze drifted to the afternoon clouds building, gray-white thunderheads piling up in the western sky. A stiff breeze was blowing, unimpeded, across the carved and eroded plateau.

"Let's rest a minute," she said, sitting down on a smooth ridge of rock. Helverson was still off in the distance, walking perilously close to the edge.

Flood put a foot up on the rock where the girl sat, and leaned both elbows on his knee. The silence flowed in around them like the fresh currents of dry air. The breeze was masking the June heat, but Flood shoved his hat off and let it hang by its lanyard down his back. The sun was hot on his face. Merliss also seemed lost in thought as she stared off into the distance. It was conceivable that the two of them might have been the last two people on the planet—maybe the only two left alive to start a new race of humans, Flood thought, his imagination running to all sorts of suppositions. If Adam and Eve actually existed, how did they feel, the only two of their species on the earth? But if one could take this portion of the Scriptures literally, God had spoken to them directly. Being alone must have seemed natural to them, since they didn't yet have the experience of other humans.

His imagination leaped backward in time, and he saw before him, not the New Mexico desert, but the Egyptian and Palestinian deserts where the first hermits had withdrawn from the world in the 4th Century to live in poverty in caves and to put God first above all else. From what he'd read of these men, they were more to be admired than imitated. To his mind, the majority of them were filthy in the extreme, eating and drinking only the minimum necessary to keep themselves alive. If the truth be known, they were eccentric when they went into isolation, and not a few of them went insane after months or years of nakedness, starvation, and harsh penances. In Flood's limited experience of this kind of life, it took a stable individual to keep his balance and perspective as a monk and, most especially, as a hermit. Prolonged solitude was strong medicine that was not the cure for everyone.

Yet, the pull of the wild desolate places was strong in him—much stronger than the attraction of civilized society. It wasn't the rigors of the eremitic life that fascinated him, however. It was a sense of being alone with God, of standing naked before Him Who drew all things to Himself with an incomprehensible love. It was trying to find Him in the tangle of one's own mind. That was the difficult part. If a hermit just sank into a comfortable, selfish existence without the bother of other people and other responsibilities, then he was worse off than before. Living as a monk or a hermit was real work, a process of trying to peel off defensive layers of pride and false images that one held up to other humans. Thinking clearly and seeing oneself clearly. That's what it was all about. And perhaps that's why he'd left the monastery. Maybe he'd just used the apparent contradiction of the Church's teaching on war and violence as an excuse to leave. The fault probably lay within himself. He couldn't face his own soul unadorned. The view was too ugly.

He squinted in the June sunlight and breathed deeply of the sage whose aroma wafted to him from the dry arroyos. He stared at the country with unseeing eyes. It didn't matter if one lived in the woods or in the desert. If a man could somehow secure enough to eat, it was mostly a matter of being relatively isolated from distractions to pursue the interior life.

"Your problem is you think too much," an old friend had once told him, when Flood was agonizing over some convoluted ethical argument. Flood could see his point, but if a person just didn't care and let things slide, what was the point of living? A man might as well exist on a natural plane, following his instincts and desires like the animals.

"What's the matter?" Merliss asked as he paced by her.

"Nothing. Just thinking."

"A penny for your thoughts," she teased.

"They're hardly worth that much," he answered. "Just a lot of mental groping."

"So you won't tell me."

Flood looked off at the distant figure of Helverson who was still poking along the cañon rim. "Maybe when we have more time," he replied.

"I wish we had a picnic lunch," she said. "It's so beautiful up here."

Flood nodded. "That would be nice. A little windy," he noted as he averted his face from the fine grit that was being blown into his eyes and nose—grit that was continuing its patient scouring and shaping of the sandstone. But the view *was* magnificent, with the white summer clouds mushrooming ever higher into the blue afternoon sky. The breeze actually felt good on his skin after the heat of the protected cañon.

He looked downstream again. Helverson was nowhere in sight. He scanned the curving cañon rim again. Maybe he'd gone down into one of the many fissures in the rock. He watched for a long minute, but the big man did not reappear.

"I don't see Helverson. Let's go find him."

He took her hand, and they began to scramble quickly over the slick, uneven rock. He didn't want the guide to reach

McGinnis before they did. Flood had learned to trust his own instinct. And his tightened stomach was telling him that Helverson meant to do the old man harm.

He wanted to let go of the woman's hand and run ahead, leaping from rock to rock, but he held himself in check and hurried at a pace that both of them could accommodate.

Flood had fixed his eyes on the spot where he'd last seen the guide. When they finally reached it, he slowed, looking. Then he spotted a cleft in the rock that couldn't be seen until they were within a few yards. The split was cluttered with boulders and rock débris that had washed down and jammed together, forming a path that only a lizard, or a very agile human, could negotiate. He heard some small rocks clattering and saw Helverson, sliding and bounding down the end of the rock slide some hundred feet below as he gained the brush-covered slope into the bottom of the cañon.

"There he goes." He took Merliss's hand again, and they started down. They clambered on hands and feet and slid on their bottoms more than they walked upright. Flood went first, picking his way carefully, yet still slipping and scraping his shins and hands several times.

By the time they reached the bottom, the guide was out of sight.

"Nice of him to wait for us," Merliss said.

"He didn't want us to come in the first place," Flood pointed out.

By the time they retrieved their horses and rejoined the guide, he was back with McGinnis. The professor was stretched out comfortably in the shade of a mesquite on the sandy bank of the stream. The guide was standing beside him.

"He says there's no place to take the horses and mules up on the cañon rim without backtracking more than a

159

day," the professor greeted them.

"Why can't we take them with us?"

"The cañon narrows down up ahead. I could see from up above that the water has gone down about as quick as it came up, but the way is blocked with a choke stone."

"A what?"

"A boulder as big as a small cabin is wedged into that narrow opening. I think we can climb over, but the animals can't. If we leave them up top, they'll be safer."

"There's almost no vegetation or shelter up there," Merliss remarked.

"Exactly," the guide nodded. "And there's no way we can get them up there anyway. I should have thought about this a couple days back."

"Yes, you should have," McGinnis said, frowning. "You're supposed to know these cañons."

The guide made no response to this.

"Well, what do you suggest?" the professor continued impatiently.

"Build a brush and rock corral and leave the animals here. Pack what we need on our backs."

"What if we have another flash flood?" Merliss asked.

"There's some benchland back there a ways that's plenty high enough, unless it rains steady for several days. They'll be safe enough and have enough to graze on for at least a few days."

"Then let's get at it," McGinnis said, getting to his feet.

"There's one more cliff dwelling that I know of about eight miles ahead," Helverson said. "If that turns out to be the one you're looking for, then we can easily make it back here the day after tomorrow."

They spent the remainder of the day building a makeshift corral. It was one that any determined mule could easily kick apart, Flood thought, but said nothing. They used an angle formed by the cañon wall, cut willows and laced them into the opening of a hastily built rock enclosure. Hauling and setting rocks was a labor Flood didn't want to repeat. By the time darkness was nearly upon them, his gloves were worn through in several spots from handling the rough rock, and his back felt as if it would break in half if he bent it one more time. He and Helverson were the last ones to quit, but Flood was satisfied with their labors. Unless they were spooked by lightning, or the water somehow rose to this height, the animals were relatively secure. A small wet weather spring still flowed from the base of the wall in sufficient quantity to keep them watered. And they were screened from view of anyone approaching from downriver. They stowed the saddles and most of the food under an overhanging ledge of rock in the cañon wall.

Each person in the party made up a pack containing only enough food for two or three days, and a dry change of clothing, matches, and their weapons. The professor added a short-handled shovel to his gear. They camped where they were, just outside the makeshift corral. Too tired to hunt, they made a stew of beans and dried beef and a few wild onions, washed down with spring water.

"I'm going to sleep out there a ways and stand guard," Flood said a half hour after supper.

Helverson and Merliss looked their question at him.

"Thought I saw some smoke when we were up on the rim today," he said. "Probably won't hurt to keep watch part of the night, at least." Before anyone could object, he hefted his Colt Lightning rifle, threw his blanket over his shoulder, and slipped away into the darkness beyond the firelight. When out of sight, he quietly circled around to the opposite side of the camp, stationed himself above the stone corral, near the cañon wall. If Helverson had a notion to do them any harm while they slept, he would have to know that Flood was out there, close by in the dark, watching and listening. Paranoid he might be, but Flood was determined not to be taken by surprise. Yet Flood had not been lying. He *had* seen some sign of dust or smoke in the distance today. And it was not a dust devil kicked up by the wind. Possibly a distant wildfire off to the north, but it looked more like a small dust cloud being churned up by horsemen.

But his move was strictly a bluff because Flood could not have kept his eyes open for more than two hours if his very life had depended on it. He slept the sleep of the dead, oblivious to any insects or prowling night creatures.

When he awoke, the wide slice of sky above the cañon was graying with dawn. He shook himself awake, picked up his blanket and rifle, and approached the camp. As he walked up, Merliss finished brushing her hair and fastened it at the base of her neck with a thin red ribbon. She had changed clothes from the mud-spattered outfit she'd been wearing the last time he saw her. "I haven't felt this grimy since I was a ten-year-old tomboy." She smiled at him. "There's some clear water from the spring to wash, but that red slurry that passes for a river is worse than useless for any kind of bathing or drinking."

"You have to strain it through your teeth." Flood grinned back at her.

"I've already got grit between my teeth . . . and in my eyes and my hair and everywhere else."

"What's for breakfast?" he asked as McGinnis emerged from the thick willows with a coffee pot filled with fresh spring water.

"Flapjacks and bacon," Helverson answered, shaking out his blanket and rolling it up. "And you'd better eat hearty because we're not taking much grub with us, unless you want to pack it yourself."

"I reckon I could let my belly go as flat as anyone else's," Flood replied easily, ignoring the peremptory tone.

"See anything last night?" Helverson asked.

"Nope." Flood shook his head.

"We need to be on the trail by sunup," Helverson said. "We've got several rough miles to cover on foot with packs."

As Flood shoveled in the limp bacon and the molasses-sweetened flapjacks, he realized he had probably lost a few pounds since leaving Santa Fé. But he'd hardened up, could spend twelve hours at a stretch in the saddle, climb up and down rocky gorges and still be ready to go the next day with little or no soreness. He thought he had become accustomed to hard work and little sleep at the monastery, but that was nothing compared to the physical strain he'd put on himself in the few weeks since he'd walked out the monastery gates.

The morning sun was lighting up the sky, but had not yet peered over the cañon rim when the four of them, Helverson in the lead, were making their way upstream along the silt-laden watercourse. Flood looked back at the horses and mules, swishing their tails and contentedly grazing inside the low stone walls of their corral. He threw his rifle into the crook of his arm and shrugged his shoulders in the straps that were already grooving his shoulders from the heavy pack. He and Helverson were carrying the mule's share of the supplies. But he could stand anything, Flood thought, if he had some hope they were nearing their goal.

At a rest break three hours later, McGinnis confided to him he thought they were getting close. While Helverson was washing his face in the stream thirty yards away, the professor replied to Flood's question by saying: "In his diary, Peter Stirling describes a passage between vertical red walls so narrow that a man on mule back could put out his arms and touch both sides of the cañon. Only a league beyond that passage is the cliff dwelling he calls the Stone Castle. That's where his party hid the treasure." His tired blue eyes lit up with the anticipation of a child on Christmas morning.

Flood merely nodded and moved away as Helverson approached.

"Let's move out," the guide said.

Chapter Fifteen

Sport of Nature

"By the Colossus of Rhodes, did you ever see anything like that?" Roddy McGinnis marveled, gazing up at the twelve-foot high boulder that blocked the narrow passage between two vertical sandstone walls. "Like a cork in a big bottle neck."

"Shows the force of water," Helverson said.

"Water?" The professor shoved his hat back on his head and arched his eyebrows. "Hell, it would take the force of Niagara Falls to move something that size."

"Right you are," the guide responded, slipping out of his pack and shoving it under the boulder where the rounded side of the stone formed a three-foot gap at the base of the vertical wall. "You can either climb over, or crawl under."

Flood noted that some water still pooled in the sandy hollow between the rock and the wall. He had an uneasy feeling about being trapped in this narrow defile if another flash flood came roaring down. Water had gushed through here within the past few hours, or the puddle would have soaked in or evaporated by now in the dry heat. He glanced at what could be seen of the sky above the high walls. Some fluffy clouds were drifting past. But there could be a deluge of rain filling the washes and gullies of the table land upstream a few miles, forming the run-off that could mean a quick, violent death for all of them if they were trapped here.

He swallowed hard and handed his pack up to Merliss who had clambered up the sloping side of the boulder. He himself opted to crawl through the triangular opening, even though it meant wetting his pants and boots. The water cooled him off. The noon sun was now boring down into the windless cañon, sucking the moisture out of their bodies.

Helverson and McGinnis also went over the rock, and the four of them gathered on the other side. A hundred yards farther, the passage was again blocked, but this time with a pile of several small boulders they had to climb over.

"How much farther does this go?" Flood grunted. The red sandstone walls were so perfectly straight up and down from the sandy floor that it appeared they were traversing an eight-foot-wide roofless hallway. Flood had a claustrophobic feeling as long as he could not see a quick way out. At least, Helverson had been telling the truth about not being able to bring the horses and mules through here.

"Another few hundred yards should do it," the guide said. "Then it opens back a ways."

Flood plodded on, following Merliss. The .44 caliber Colt Lightning rifle with its long, octagonal barrel was getting heavier every hour. His loaded pistol was still strapped to his hip, and he almost wished he'd left the heavy long gun with his horse. He doubted that he'd need both. Was he expecting a gun battle or a siege of some kind? He smiled to himself. Maybe it was because he was embarrassed to admit to Merliss that he couldn't hit a moving target as small as a rattlesnake or a jack rabbit with a handgun. Yet he'd promised in Santa Fé to show Merliss how to shoot a pistol. So far, he'd neglected to keep that promise. He assumed she still carried the loaded Smith & Wesson pocket pistol. He didn't remember seeing her clean or dry the weapon after their soaking in the river. He resolved to ask her about it the first time he caught her away from the others.

They had to scramble over one more obstacle, this time a jumble of rocks the size of horses that jammed the narrow cañon to a height of about eight feet. Then the walls began to fall away on either side, and the more familiar sandbars and willows appeared, then the higher sandy loam leading up to the broken perpendicular walls.

Another mile brought them around a slight bend, and Helverson stopped.

"There it is," he said, pointing at a wide slash in the cañon wall about halfway up.

They all stopped and stared. A cluster of stone and mud structures seemed to fill the gash from side to side. In spite of the heat, Flood felt a chill go over him at the brooding silence of the place. The black squares of windows and doors stared out at the cañon with empty eyes, just as they had for more than a hundred generations. How many ghosts of the vanished builders still inhabited the place, guarding it against enemy intruders just as those first Indians had done? But guarding what? A treasure no one could calculate?

With an effort, Flood pulled his gaze away to break the spell. Above the cave, the lighter sandstone was marked with vertical black streaks where centuries of run-off from the rim had stained the rock. From this distance, he saw no obvious way up to the cave above the green vegetation that cloaked the opposite shore of the nearly dry riverbed. Measuring with his eyes, he guessed the lip of the cave was more than a hundred feet above the bottom of the gorge where they stood.

The breeze that was driving the puffy white clouds overhead now reached down to them, drying the sweat under Flood's shirt. He was suddenly conscious of being very thirsty.

"Let's find some shade and have something to eat before

we tackle that," McGinnis said, breaking the silence. Flood noticed the professor's eyes were bright with the anticipation of opening a present.

As Flood gathered sticks of dry driftwood for a fire, he wondered if the last white men to make footprints in the sand of this gorge might have been Peter Stirling's party three and half centuries earlier. In the partial shade of a large mesquite bush, they fried bacon, ate dry biscuits, and boiled some coffee to wash it down. Flood was hardly aware of what he was eating. As he squatted on his heels with the tin plate, his gaze was pulled toward the waiting cliff dwelling. The cave opening faced southwest and was beginning to catch the full light of the early afternoon sun.

There was little conversation. Flood eyed both Helverson and McGinnis. Was the professor going to confide in the guide? Or would he wait until it was clear about whether or not there was a treasure? If they came up empty, McGinnis did not seem the type who wanted to look like a fool in front of this stranger.

Lunch ended, and the utensils were cleaned and stowed. They started again, and Flood took advantage of bringing up the rear to check the loads and action of his Colt Bisley. He carried the rifle with a full magazine. They crossed the small stream and plunged into the willows bordering it. Then they were out and climbing over gravel and loose shale, dodging prickly pear cacti and stunted cedars.

Flood inhaled deeply of the fragrance of the gray-green sage. In the bright afternoon sun the green of the cedars and cottonwoods made a beautiful, cool contrast to the hot red of the sandstone cliffs. As they climbed toward the cave, Flood thought it appeared much larger than he'd estimated from a distance.

This time they did not have to search for a way up. It was a very rough slope and required slow going, but the tumbled boulders and rocks and sand had washed down to form a slope that led to the lip of the lower end of the cave. An ancient retaining wall had been constructed along the front edge of the cave, jutting up two feet above the floor. The four of them stumbled into the dusty cavern and paused. Except for the wind sighing in the trees below, their harsh breathing was the only sound.

"This look like the place, Professor?" Helverson broke the silence.

"I'll have to look around a little," McGinnis said. "The Gallina people didn't build apartments. Their buildings are separate and individual." He moved quickly to scramble over the piles of fallen rock walls that littered the floor everywhere, especially toward the front of the deep cave. "They mostly built on tops of mesas where they had a clear view of the countryside," McGinnis went on. "And they dug lots of pit houses. Their cliff dwellings were mostly for storage and defense. Keep an eye out for any pottery. They have a unique style."

The professor was not a convincing liar, Flood thought, eyeing Helverson. McGinnis's enthusiasm for finding a rare cliff dwelling of the Gallina people sounded forced. But maybe that was because Flood knew it was only a cover. Keeping the big guide in view, Flood gripped his rifle and walked toward the front of the cave by the retaining wall. He pretended to be looking out toward the cañon floor below.

"My late colleague said their dwellings were laid out with a fire pit, heat deflector, and ventilator shaft," McGinnis said, his voice becoming slightly muffled as he ducked his head to enter one of the low, T-shaped doorways into a room. "Yes. Yes, here are the symmetrically paired storage bins against the back wall, and the benches, just like he said."

"Do you see any signs that your friend was here?" Flood asked, trying to perpetuate the charade.

"No. He wrote that he'd made no marks and even brushed out his footprints in the dust before he left," the professor said.

Flood noticed the notched logs still leaning against the buildings and providing access through the roofs to the second-story rooms.

Merliss was wandering through the buildings and climbing over the rubble of partially fallen stone walls. Unlike the other cliff dwellings they'd visited so far, this one was definitely constructed differently. The rooms were built separately from each other instead of adjoining. Flat paving stones even covered the floor of the cave, and the mostly intact sandstone rooms were plastered with mud.

"The floor back there by the storage bin is littered with hundreds of little corn cobs," Merliss said, emerging from a low doorway. "I even found a child's footprint in the dried mud. Looked like it had just been made yesterday."

She came toward Flood. He moved aside to keep Helverson in sight, hardly hearing what she was saying. The guide was sitting on a pile of fallen stones, carbine across his knees. From all appearances, he was bored as he rolled and struck a match to a cigarette. But Flood noted the eyes under the hooded lids, darting here and there, squinting through the smoke, mostly following the movements of the professor.

In front of the row of dwellings, Flood saw two kivas, the circular, rock-lined pits sunk into the floor of the cave. One of them appeared half filled with débris from its caved-in roof— poles, dirt, and stone. The other, about a dozen feet in diameter, was still roofed. The crooked poles, criss-crossed to form a mat and covered with dried mud, seemed, to Flood's inexpert eyes, to be of slightly different workmanship and design, than the rest of its ancient surroundings.

Merliss was pulling her Kodak out of the pack she had put down. "The sun is at a perfect angle to get some pictures," she said, winding the film. "These lovely, old ruins seem like they were just vacated a day or two ago . . . as if the Indians might come back at any time." She ran her hand over the wall's surface. "You can still see the finger marks of the builders in this mud plaster." She stepped up on the low rock retaining wall and held the box camera in front of her, looking down into the viewfinder. She snapped the shutter, then wound the film for another shot, as she stepped down and moved away a few feet. "The sun makes these yellow and red rocks almost glow," she said, trying to frame another picture. "You know, I forget about having this camera," she said. "I wish I'd remembered to take some pictures as we went along."

Flood thought about the early incident along the Río Grande when the guide had reacted almost violently to Merliss's taking a snapshot of him.

"I think there's even enough light to get a photo of those pictographs painted on the back wall," she said.

"Pictographs?" Flood asked.

"Yes. Some sort of yellow, circular designs. Maybe the sun, maybe sunflowers. There are also some birds that seem to be flying in formation. Look like herons or cranes. Come on. I'll show you."

"Not just now," he said, still eyeing Helverson.

McGinnis emerged from the doorway of the last room at the far end of the two-hundred-foot-long cave. His white hair was in wild disarray as he slid down a pile of rock débris, stirring up a small cloud of dust. He came toward them, unmindful of the dust that coated his jacket and pants the color of his sunburned face and hands. He yanked a short-handled shovel from his pack on the ground and jabbed it into the pile of loose stone and dirt, then picked up his canteen, and took a good drink. He wiped his stubbled chin with the back of his hand. "I was saving the best till last," he winked, dropping his voice. "By the golden dome of Saint Peter's, if the stuff isn't in that sealed kiva, then I'm not an archaeologist."

"What if you find only a few dusty skeletons?" Flood asked, trying to soften the blow of a potential let-down.

"No. That's not a burial chamber. Those willow branches are laid in a different pattern. And, besides, if the Gallina people had constructed it, they would have left an opening for a ladder. And it's not a grain storage bin. Several of those are built against the back wall. This kiva has been tampered with."

"How can you tell, Uncle Mac?" Merliss asked. "It's so dry in this country, that everything looks like it was made last year, instead of centuries ago. Nothing decays."

"I'm not an expert on the Pueblo Indians. But when you've been at this as long as I have, you notice small details." He took a deep breath and picked up his shovel. "Give me a hand breaking into this kiva," he said to Flood. "Merliss can get our picture."

"Go ahead," Flood said, swinging the rifle into the crook of his arm. "I don't want to steal any of your thunder." Out of the corner of his eye, he could see Helverson, still seated on the rock pile, grind out his cigarette under his heel.

Merliss and her uncle moved toward the sealed kiva, and the old man jabbed the point of the shovel into the crusty brown layer of dried mud that plastered the top of the underground chamber. Several more jabs and it began to crumble.

Flood moved to the opposite side of the dig, pretending to be watching McGinnis chop his way through the plastered web of saplings. But he was tensely observing the guide through slitted eyes. He saw Helverson casually stand up and sidle toward the corner of one of the stone structures, about thirty feet closer to the three of them.

Merliss, apparently not sensing any danger, was wiping the lens of her Kodak with her shirt tail. Flood hoped his premonition was completely wrong, but he had come to trust his instincts, and every nerve was screaming at him that deadly danger was all around them. It was almost as if he could smell electricity in the air.

McGinnis continued to dig, knocking the dried mud loose in chunks, then pausing to tear the woven saplings apart, flinging them behind him. Merliss was tinkering with her camera, moving to one side so her shadow would not be in the photograph.

McGinnis, holding the shovel in one hand, lowered himself through a three-foot opening he'd finally managed to rip in the lid of the kiva. He sank only as far as his waist. Then he ducked under the remaining covering, and Flood could hear him grunting as he rummaged around in the dimness of the pit.

"By the head of the golden calf!" he croaked, popping his torso out of the hole like a jack-in-the-box. "Feast your eyes on this!" He held up the golden figurine of a cat that looked decidedly Egyptian. The afternoon sun shone on the emeralds that formed the cat's eyes. In his other hand, McGinnis held up an ornamental gold chain. "I'm standing on at least a ton of gold," he breathed in an awe-filled voice, as if the find had sucked all the air out of his lungs.

In spite of himself, Flood turned to look. In that instant, he heard the camera shutter click behind him and caught a slight movement out of the corner of his eye from thirty feet away.

With a reflex, he swung the rifle down from the crook of

his arm, yanking the slide back and forward just as the barrel came level with his hip. The muzzle jetted flame at the same moment that Helverson fired. The two shots roared as one. Helverson's hat went flying, and he dived for cover.

"Down!" Flood yelled, jacking another round into the chamber and lunging forward, stumbling over the piled dirt in his haste. A bullet cut a groove in the sandstone beside him, whining off into the cañon. Flood rolled over and fired again, but his target was gone. The crashing of the heavy-caliber rifles was slamming back and forth from the walls. The concussion temporarily deafened him, and he had to rely on his eyes alone. Two shots blasted from the doorway of a room several yards away. The shooter did not expose himself, and the shots were fired blindly. But one of the slugs threw rock dust into Flood's eyes. Now his vision was blurred as well, and he rolled to one side, sharp rocks digging into his ribs. He blinked the tears away, trying to clear his vision, knowing that he was still exposed. But he dared not turn away to find a place to hide while Helverson was in front of him. The guide would have to show at least part of himself to get a shot at him now. Flood's heart was hammering and his ears ringing from the explosions, but he held the rifle steady, hammer cocked.

After the first fusillade, a nervous silence fell. Where was Helverson? Flood's eyes scanned the stone structures in front, then left and right. He gripped his rifle with sweaty palms. He wanted to find out where Merliss and McGinnis were, but dared not yell or turn to look. Not while Helverson was stalking them. Then he heard two quick shots from behind him and turned his head just enough to see Merliss holding her Smith & Wesson with both hands and firing toward the hidden guide. She flinched as she fired a third shot.

Flood faced front just in time to see a flicker of movement about fifty yards away. It was only a flash, and, before he could focus on the spot, it was gone. But he heard stones rattle as someone went down the trail and knew Helverson had made good his escape from the far end of the cave. Now he was outside and could hold them at bay from cover anywhere below.

"Damn," Flood muttered to himself, his heart still thudding heavily in his chest. He half turned. "Merliss," he called softly. "Thanks for the help. You two all right?"

"No. He got Uncle Mac. Where's Helverson?"

"He's gone out the other end." He crabbed backward to the kiva, staying behind a jumble of rocks.

"He was trying to kill us," she almost sobbed. "He shot Uncle Mac."

Flood's stomach contracted, fearing the worst. He looked down into the dim interior where she was cradling the professor's head. He saw blood on her blouse and hands and the bandanna she pressed to McGinnis's face.

"I can't see for all this blood, but I don't think it broke his jaw or his skull. Looks like it cut a groove along his jawbone," she said, wiping the bright red blood from the short, white whiskers. "An inch to the left and he'd probably be dead." She looked up at Flood with tear-filled eyes. "He's just stunned. Uncle Mac! Uncle Mac! Wake up! Say something! If I can just get this bleeding stopped. . . ."

Flood heard the strained self-control in her voice. His eyes adjusted to the dim light, and he saw the professor's eyes. They had a glazed, faraway look. If he was conscious and knew what had happened, he gave no indication of it. Flood took a deep breath. One second McGinnis had been on top of his career, overflowing with jubilation, the ancient treasure of the Templars beneath his feet. The next second he'd been cut

175

down by an attempted assassination.

"If you hadn't fired at the same time, Uncle Mac would have been killed," she said. "How did you know he was going to shoot us?" She looked up at him with anguish in her blue eyes.

"I didn't," he replied huskily. "But I suspected he was up to something." He swung his legs over the edge of the kiva and, with a searching look around for their assailant, let himself down. He gently pulled the woman's hand away and took a quick look at the wound. Just as she'd said. Not fatal, unless it became infected later. Just painful and bloody. It remained to be seen if the jawbone or any teeth were damaged.

Maybe the guide would be back to finish them, so the wound wouldn't have a chance to heal or mortify. Was it possible they were all going to leave their bones atop this treasure, after coming so far to find it? Not if he had breath in his body.

She looked at him, and her steely resolve nearly cracked. "Marc, what are we going to do?"

He carefully poked his head up out of the pit and looked around. The westering sun was sliding down behind a cloud bank in a welter of red and gold. Night would be coming on in a few hours, and a killer was out there waiting for them—a killer who knew the terrain and had them trapped, probably watching the cave at this moment. With his element of surprise gone in the first few seconds, there was no reason for Helverson needlessly to expose himself to their guns, when he could easily wait them out. Flood's stomach contracted into a cold knot with the realization of their predicament.

Chapter Sixteen

Requiem

Nothing in his previous experience had prepared him for this. Flood ducked back into the kiva. He took a deep breath to steady himself, knowing that Merliss was looking to him for direction, as she pressed the bandanna against her uncle's jaw. Her eyes were wide in the dimness, but Flood felt their question.

"You and Mac stay here in the kiva for now," he said. "At least, until it gets dark."

"Wouldn't it be better if we get out of this cave?" she asked.

Flood shook his head. "He knows this country. We can't travel as fast as he can since we'd have to help your injured uncle. Helverson could slip up and ambush us anywhere out there in the trees and undergrowth." He paused. "I'll get our packs and drag them back into one of those rooms. We can risk a fire when we're behind a stone wall. I'll find a good defensible position in a room where there's more than one way out."

Before she could reply, he slipped out of the pit and went to collect the packs each of them had shed when they entered the cave. Keeping behind the crumbled outer walls as much as possible, he darted here and there, holding his rifle in one hand and snatching up the small makeshift packs with the other. He was disappointed to see that Helverson had apparently grabbed up his own pack when he made good his escape. Knowing who Helverson really was and what he planned to do were crucial to preparing any defense against him. If the man just wanted to leave them stranded, he could have done so at any time before they reached this cave. So Flood assumed Helverson would not just hike back to the horses and leave. He'd waited until McGinnis found the treasure to kill them.

He straightened up, dragging the three packs in one hand. The boom of a heavy caliber rifle shocked the silence, and a slug sprayed chips from the stone wall behind him. He sprawled forward and lay still, breathing hard, hugging the hard stone floor behind the partial cover of the tumbled rock wall. Helverson had him in his sights, probably from the cover of those trees about a hundred yards away and below him. Well, that answered his question about the guide's intentions.

Flood squirmed to bring his rifle to bear and barely lifted his eyes above the edge of the rock pile. Smokeless powder and the leaves of the foliage had effectively dissipated any telltale signs of smoke. Flood guessed the general area of where the shot might have come from and fired, worked the slide, and fired again, a few yards to one side, the brass butt plate bucking slightly against his shoulder. The empty brass shell casing tinkled on the rocks as he worked the slide to chamber another round. *At least, the bastard knows he didn't get me,* Flood thought. He waited several seconds, picked out a doorway about twenty feet away, then got his feet under him, crouched, and made a rush for it. Another shot came from outside, and Flood heard the bullet slam into the mud plaster of the wall as he dived through the open doorway, dragging the packs. He lay there, panting and fighting the sharp pain of a shin banged against the rock door sill.

He sat up behind the protection of the wall and decided this room would be a good place to make a stand. Unlike other cliff dwellings they had explored, this one was not built with connecting rooms. Each structure here was free standing, with spaces between. This one still had its ceiling of closely placed cedar poles and a notched log ladder lay on the ground just outside the door, apparently to provide access to the upper floor.

He slipped off his hat and edged it around the doorway. When it didn't draw fire, he slid one eye past the opening. He had a wide view of the river cañon below. The problem was that the man could be hiding anywhere in those cedars, or the willows that choked the sandbars along the stream. He pulled his head back and sat down with his back against the wall to consider his next move. He had a rifle, a pistol, and about fifty extra cartridges that would fit either. As far as he knew, McGinnis was unarmed, but the professor wouldn't be much good in a fight even if he weren't injured. Merliss had both a pistol and the grit to use it. He wondered if she'd brought any extra ammunition in her pack. They could make a stand here. But for how long? Water would be the problem, if Helverson decided to lay siege and wait them out.

He took another peek. The sun had dropped farther behind the massing dark clouds in the west, and dusk was creeping into the cañon. He had to get back to Merliss. He knew she'd heard the gunfire and would be wondering. But at least she had the good sense not to cry out. He stacked the packs against the wall, edged out the side door of the room, and, wormed along on his belly another thirty feet to the lip of the kiva.

"Merliss, don't shoot. It's me," he whispered hoarsely.

"Oh, Marc. What's going on?" She gripped her Smith & Wesson.

"He's out there, somewhere, taking shots at me," Flood said, as he dropped to a crouch inside the circular pit. "How is he?" he nodded toward McGinnis who lay on his back with his eyes closed. The left side of his face was a mass of blood.

"I've managed to get the bleeding stopped, but he must have a concussion," she replied. "At first, I thought he was just stunned, like someone had hit him on the jaw with a fist. But apparently it was a much harder blow."

"It'll be dark soon. We can move him back to that room where I've got the packs. We can better care for him there. How much water do you have left in your canteen?"

She slipped it off her shoulder and shook it. "Maybe a quart. I used some of it to clean the blood off his face."

"Save the rest. Before we're out of here, it may be more precious than this gold we're sitting on."

"Marc, is he going to come back and kill us?" She blinked away the tears.

Suddenly smitten, he reached out and covered her hand with his. "Don't worry. If we keep our heads about us and just think about what we have to do, we'll be all right." He hadn't answered her question, but she knew the answer. She just needed a little reassurance.

He carefully raised his head above the rim of the kiva. The long dusk of summer was coming on. He scanned the cave from one end to the other. There was no movement, no sound. Helverson was no Apache. He had neither the stalking skills nor the patience of one. Physically he was a bigger, stronger man, but Flood was confident that with a rifle or pistol he was at least the guide's equal. It was his own resolve he worried about. Except in the heat of self-preservation, he doubted he could shoot another human being, so that would probably eliminate gunning down Helverson if he got a clear shot at him from ambush.

180

Now was the time to move, with the shadows of night beginning to fill the cañon. A distant sniper would have a difficult time picking out his targets. "Let's go," he whispered. He and Merliss lifted the unconscious man out of the treasure hole. "Follow me," he said. "Crawl as low as you can." Flood noted that her jacket concealed the dirty white of her blouse, making her less conspicuous. He took the old man under the shoulders and, crouching, walked backward, dragging him between the stone buildings and into the side door of the room.

"There are some matches in my pack," he said to Merliss. "I'm going to find something to start a fire."

"Do you think it's safe to show a light?" she asked.

"Yes. If I can find enough wood, I'll start a couple more fires in those other rooms. After we get something in our stomachs, we'll move away from the fires and keep watch. If he has any ideas about coming in here after us, he'll have to check each fire. By then we should spot him."

"Oh, Marc, I'm so afraid! This is like some horrible nightmare."

"We'll get through it, all right. Don't worry. Just do as I say."

He handed her the rifle and moved away quickly into the darkness, wondering if his words sounded convincing. He had no reason for optimism, but he assessed their chances at least as even.

He knocked the dirt loose from the broken top of the kiva and dragged the dry saplings and poles back to Merliss. "Don't start the fire yet," he cautioned her. "Let me find some more timbers to burn."

This time he found the professor's short shovel and, using the last of the light, rummaged around in two of the other rooms for branches and timbers from collapsed roofs. It took him the better part of a half hour, but he finally got three fires going in different rooms. He was heedless of the noise he made but was careful not to show himself toward the front of the cave against the firelight. He piled on some large logs to be sure they burned a long time, but, where they sat with McGinnis, he started only a small blaze, large enough to cook over and to provide a little light, but not big enough to blind them. He dug a can of beans from a pack and haggled it open with the professor's knife. They fried bacon and ate some dry bread. Flood used some of the precious water from a canteen to make a half pot of coffee, thinking that he might need it to stay awake and on guard this night. His stomach was tight, and he had trouble eating at first. But as the hours passed, he began to relax, thinking that Helverson was not going to try a night attack.

To cheer him further, McGinnis regained consciousness. He was still groggy, and his jaw was so swollen and sore he could hardly open his mouth. But he was coherent and was able to take some nourishment in the form of sweetened coffee and some mashed beans.

"What happened?" he managed to articulate as Merliss held a tin cup for him to sip.

"Helverson tried to kill you, and probably would have shot all of us," Flood answered.

"Why?"

"I wish I could answer that." He looked at the scabbing wound along the professor's jaw. The half-inch white stubble had been plowed up like a patch of frosty grass. "Wish I had some whisky to clean that up."

"By the blood of the martyrs, if I had some whisky, I wouldn't be wasting it on this face," the professor croaked.

Good, Flood thought. The old man seemed to be his old self.

Merliss had made a pillow and backrest from the canvas packs. "Uncle Mac, why don't you just lie back and try to rest?" she urged. "You'll feel better in the morning."

"Whew! I never had a head like this," he murmured, closing his eyes. "Feels as big around as that kiva." He managed a crooked grin. "But I was right about that treasure! I was right! I'll be famous! I showed those doubting bastards!" His voice trailed off, and the grin faded, as he drifted into a doze.

Flood sat quietly until the steady breathing told him the old man was asleep and beyond distress for the moment. The dry, popping cedar poles were burning low, and he slid them back from the fire. Taking its fuel allowed the blaze gradually to flicker and die down to glowing coals. The smoke of the aromatic cedar and piñon pine brought back a strong, unbidden memory of incense. The darkness around them was replaced in his mind's eye by the brightly lit interior of the Gothic church at Gethsemani, Kentucky. Candles flickered everywhere on the high altar, and a robed monk was swinging a silver censer that billowed fragrant white smoke while the monks' choir sang the *Requiem*. Strong, male voices filled the tall, narrow nave with tones of ancient Gregorian chant. *"Requiem æternam dona eis, Domine, et lux perpetua luceat eis. . . ."* The familiar chant rose and fell like a smooth river of sound. Whose *Requiem* Mass were they celebrating? One of the monks had died. A robed body lay on the open wooden bier in the center aisle, flanked on either side by three tall candles. Flood was not in the church or the choir stalls; he was somehow suspended above them, floating over the scene, observing it all. He had taken part in funeral Masses many times, and there was something very comforting about it as they bid their brother good bye—the movement of the celebrant, the responses of the choir.

Dies iræ, dies illa,
Solvet sæclum in favilla,
Teste David cum Sybylla.

With no effort at all, he drifted down closer through the incense-scented air until he could see the corpse clearly. It was his own youthful face! A sudden chill went over him, and the music faded in his ears.

"Marc! Marc!" The low, insistent voice, speaking his name and the hand on his bare wrist changed the scene suddenly. He opened his eyes and blinked twice. Darkness. Was it the Angel of Death calling him? He tried to move, but felt heavy, earthbound.

"Do you want me to keep watch first?" It was Merliss's voice.

"Oh!" he gasped. "What a nightmare." He rubbed his face, trying to erase the vivid scene. He'd been asleep. Well, so much for the stimulating effects of the coffee. The dream slowly faded. In place of the chant in his head came a low, moaning sound from the front of the cave. "Wind's coming up," he said.

"I hear it," she said. "Must be a storm brewing somewhere. I can see lightning now and then off in the distance."

"I'll keep watch first," he said quietly. He feared, if he slept again, the dream might not only recur, it might come true—if Helverson somehow crept up on them.

"You're tired," she insisted. "Why don't you stay here and sleep? I'll wake you. I'm so nervous, I can't sleep."

"Tell you what," he proposed, feeling for the rifle against the wall, "come outside with me and we'll talk to keep me awake. With this wind kicking up, our voices won't be heard." He took her hand, and, leaving the professor asleep in the darkened room by the glowing coals of the fire, they

184

crept out a few yards to the low retaining wall along the mouth of the cave.

They sat by a V-shaped break in the masonry where Flood could scan the area in front without exposing any part of himself in case the two decoy fires he'd set were backlighting them. The wind was keening louder around an edge of rock somewhere along the huge overhang above them.

Flood took a look through the break in the wall, but the darkness was complete. He pulled back from the opening and leaned against the wall. "Trouble with this wind, it not only masks our voices, it also covers any sounds he makes down below," Flood remarked. He heard the tops of the cottonwoods thrashing with a sound like rushing water and could smell the dust being kicked up from the arid cañon floor. Somewhere in the middle distance heat lightning flickered.

Merliss leaned against the rock and hugged her jacket tightly around herself. They sat in silence for a few seconds. Finally she said: "Why is Helverson trying to kill us?"

"That's the big question." Flood sighed. "I don't think this was a quick decision after he saw the treasure. I'd bet he's one of those who've been trying to murder your uncle all along."

"A Templar?"

"Right. It seems a little too coincidental that Mac just happened to meet a man in that Santa Fé saloon who was ready, willing, and able to guide us to these ruins. And just at the precise moment that we needed a guide."

"Coincidences do happen," she reminded him. "Life forces in the universe sometimes cross at random."

"Not to my way of thinking," he said. "Providence, maybe. Coincidence, never."

"Well, whatever you call it, it's something that couldn't be predicted," she said.

"In this instance, I'd say it was planned . . . by Helverson, or someone above him. Somehow we didn't completely shake those Templars off our trail, and this one was there to meet us in Santa Fé."

"He could have killed us there and probably gotten away with it," Merliss mused. "Saved himself a lot of trouble."

"No. It would have caused a lot of trouble. Too many people around and he could have been caught and exposed. Also, no place to easily dispose of the bodies . . . not like out in this wilderness. But he wanted to bring those two friends of his who were probably Templars, too."

"You're right. Then he tried to make our deaths appear accidental . . . like that fall down the cañon wall when he let go of Uncle Mac and almost killed us all."

"And what Helverson claimed was a shot at a snake the other day that nearly got Mac in the head," Flood added.

"He was taking a big chance that he could find the treasure by himself, just with Uncle Mac's notes."

Flood nodded. "That's probably why he finally let the professor lead him to it, then gave up all pretense of causing an *accident*. As soon as we were distracted and excited by the find, he tried to gun us down."

"Lucky you were watching."

"I was too slow. I should have trusted my instincts and disarmed him just as we came into this cave," Flood said bitterly. "But I wasn't certain. Now he's got us in a box." He paused, not wanting to alarm her any more than she already was. But he was on the verge of panic himself. And he needed her support and comfort as well. He scrubbed a hand across his face and felt the fine dust and the lengthening stubble. He quelled the fear rising in his stomach, wiped his sweaty palms on his dirty Levi's, then gripped the rifle, and wormed his way to the notch in the wall. This time he waited for another flash of heat lightning that seemed to be getting closer. The dim light provided by the momentary flash showed him only the trees and bushes, the sandbars near the trickle of river, and the glimpse of red cliffs across the cañon about two hundred yards away. He watched for several minutes but saw no sign of human or animal. He would have been very surprised if he had. He sat back against the wall and laid his hat beside him, feeling the breeze stir his sweaty hair.

What was done was past, and he had to keep his wits about him and try to think like Helverson would think if they were to get out of this alive. If the guide *was* a Templar assassin, as now appeared very likely, then he had been sent by someone in higher authority. He would have to report back that he had either succeeded or failed. If he failed, and lost the treasure to some outsiders, he would surely face execution. So, Flood reasoned, Helverson would either let them go and flee for his life from Templar vengeance, or he would give his life in an all-out attempt to kill the three of them and keep the treasure. Flood tried to guess which course the man would take. Helverson was a taciturn individual, but was he a fanatic underneath, dedicated to a cause from which he would never consider retreat? Flood had to assume the latter. He doubted that a monastic warrior order as old and powerful as the Knights Templar would have entrusted the finding of their vast treasure to any man who was something less than rabidly dedicated to their cause. So Flood had to operate on the premise that the guide would continue trying to kill them with all the strength and cunning at his command. Now the only question that remained was whether Helverson would try to attack under cover of darkness and the noise of the approaching storm, or would he simply wait somewhere out there, with plenty of food and water and cover and starve them out?

Flood's initial reaction had been so swift, he wondered if

the guide even knew he'd wounded McGinnis. If he had to guess, Flood thought Helverson would take the patient approach. After all, no one knew where they had gone. They had seen no other humans after they'd turned west from the Río Grande. It would be relatively easy and quick to let thirst drive them out of hiding. By his estimation, all three of their canteens, since he'd brewed a quart of coffee, held no more than three pints of water, total. In this heat and with a wounded man who'd lost some blood, that water would last the three of them no more than a day, even with rationing.

"Did you get a good look at that treasure?" he asked.

"Only a few pieces," she replied.

"Is it really worth all this?"

He could almost hear the smile in her voice. "Depends on your values, don't you think?"

"Yes. Your uncle would say it's worth even being wounded, but not because of the value of the treasure. Appears to me, he just wants the fame for discovering it."

"I don't know how any individuals or organizations could prove it was theirs. So, if Uncle Mac wants to claim ownership by right of salvage, who's to dispute it?"

"The Templars might fight it in court, but they'd have to expose their order to do it. Since it's on federal land, the U.S. government would probably want a big hunk."

The lightning was flickering intermittently, reflecting from the stone buildings in the cave.

"This place is eerie," she said, huddling next to the wall and watching the light display.

"Have you got some matches with you?" he asked.

"Yes."

"Why don't you make some kind of torch and take a look at that treasure?" he suggested, hoping to distract her from their situation.

"It can wait," she replied simply. "It's been here a long time. It'll be here tomorrow." Her voice sounded tired.

They fell silent for a time, listening to the rising and falling moan of the wind around the angles of rock. The next time Flood spoke to her, he got no reply. He looked closely and saw she was lying on her side next to the wall, asleep. Surprisingly he was still alert. Should he let her sleep, or wake her and send her back to be near McGinnis in case he awoke?

He took a look through the broken wall. As far as he could tell, the valley was devoid of human life. He knew better. He would stay still and try to remain alert. Let Helverson make a move if he would. The guide would not see Flood until it was too late. He had a feeling Helverson would not come in the dark; he would play it safe and get them later. Flood relaxed. A brilliant flash of lightning made his heart leap. A crash of thunder followed, reverberating through the rocky cave. Then sheets of rain began slashing down, blowing a chilling spray over them. He woke Merliss gently.

"Oh, I was having such a nice dream," she groaned. "I was at home, teaching my students. The grass and trees were green and. . . ."

"Better get back in there with your uncle," he said, his mouth close to her ear. "Keep him warm and dry. The longer he can sleep, the better. He'll be hurting like hell when he wakes up. Go on now. If I can't stay awake, I'll come and get you to relieve me." He had no intention of doing so but wanted her to know he'd be depending on her. If Helverson was peacefully sleeping in some rocky recess out of the weather, he would be fresh come daylight, and Flood would need her eyes and ears and maybe her gun as well.

He wished Mac had not been wounded, or they might have attempted to escape under cover of the storm. But it was not to be. He had to play the hand he was dealt. He didn't believe in premonitions, or the sight of his own dead body in his dream might have profoundly disturbed him.

Chapter Seventeen

Libera Animas Omnium Fidelum

Flood blinked his eyes at the gray light filtering into the cave and felt a moment of panic when he realized he'd been asleep. The night had passed in a long agony of fighting drowsiness. If Helverson had chosen to attack, Flood would have almost certainly been taken by surprise, so groggy had he been even during his wakeful periods.

He quickly thrust what might have been behind him. He had survived the night, and he stretched stiff, cold muscles. The cañon below was growing lighter by the minute, but he noted, after rubbing his eyes and taking a close look through the notch in the wall, there was still no sign of movement.

He gripped the rifle and crept backward to the side doorway of the stone room and found both McGinnis and Merliss asleep, huddled together, and the fire out. He stirred the ashes and found a hot coal deep underneath, then coaxed a flame from it with the shreds of bark from some of the cedar poles. A few minutes later he was nourishing a small blaze as Merliss awoke.

"How is he?" Flood nodded toward the professor.

"Woke up in a lot of pain, but I finally got him settled down again."

"Never seem to have any whisky when you need it, much

less any carbolic or other disinfectant. The whole side of his face is swollen," he observed, feeding the fire with larger slivers of wood he was whittling from one of the poles.

"I doubt if he can even open his mouth," she said, gazing down at her uncle who was just stirring to wakefulness.

The professor groaned and put a hand tentatively to his jaw where dried blood encrusted his white whiskers. He mumbled something unintelligible.

"Heat some water and soak his face," Flood said. "Might limber it up and make him feel better. Use what water's left to boil coffee. We'll all need some."

"That will finish the water," she said.

"Won't matter. One way or another we'll be out of here today. I'm not sitting in this cave to let him decide what will happen."

"What are you going to do?"

"As soon as we get some food under our belts, we're hiking out of here."

"What about . . . ?"

"We'll just have to take our chances. He could easily wait us out since we'll be getting mighty thirsty by tomorrow."

"I started to ask you about the treasure."

"Without pack mules there's no way we can haul it out of here. We'll spread it out on the ground, and you can take some photographs of it as soon as the light is strong enough. Maybe stuff a few of the lighter gold pieces into one of the packs. That's all for now. We'll just cover it up in the kiva and have to come back later."

She nodded thoughtfully as she poured water from her canteen into the coffee pot.

He glanced down at her. "You've got some red mud on your neck," he said absently.

Her hand flew to her neck, and she quickly turned up the

collar of her blouse. Her face reddened as she looked away and poked at the fire.

"What's wrong?" he asked, squatting down. "Are you hurt? Is that a cut?"

She shook her head, still without looking at him. "No. It's a birthmark."

He wondered why he hadn't noticed it before, then recalled that the bandanna she'd used to wipe Mac's face had been worn around her neck. She was obviously embarrassed by the mark. He didn't understand why. On impulse, he leaned over and kissed her cheek. "Did you know courtly French women used to wear fake moles as beauty marks?" he asked. "You don't need a beauty mark, but I like it."

She reddened still further, but flicked her eyes at him in a quick sign of gratitude.

"I'll start dragging the treasure up and spreading it out on the ground while you're fixing some food and helping him," he said.

He took the rifle and slipped outside again. He swept the cave with the rifle barrel, eyes alert to any movement as he crept to the retaining wall. Nothing. It wouldn't do to get careless. Helverson could be hiding in those trees, just waiting for an easy shot.

Staying under cover, Flood went to the kiva and let himself down inside. The treasure, in leather sacks, filled the bottom of the pit to an unknown depth. The knotted tie straps on the topmost sack broke off in his hand. Looking inside, he caught his breath. Even in the early morning light, the contents of the heavy bag seemed to glow with a dull golden light. He plunged a hand into a pile of loose coins and let them slide through his fingers with a metallic clinking. He picked up two or three of the silver coins and looked closer at them. They contained the image of some long-forgotten

193

Roman emperor. He recognized some Arabic writing on several others. Ruby-encrusted necklaces, bracelets, gold and silver salvers, and ornaments of all kinds filled the bag, along with brooches and pins to hold cloaks and golden cups, some with Latin inscriptions. Gold and silver crosses of various sizes and designs were in abundance, along with many crudely smelted small gold bars.

Flood wrestled the bag aside. The edges of several others peeked from under the pile. He tugged at them. Heavier than sacks of wet sand. Apparently the only thing limiting the size of the leather pouches was the weight each of them had to carry. The leather smelled musty and was dried out, breaking apart as he pulled on the sacks. Plainly it could not be transported out of here in the dry rotten bags. The treasure had outlasted its hide containers.

Gold was as close as a changing world would ever come to a material constant. It never rusted or tarnished. It did not rot or deteriorate in any natural way. It could be fashioned into countless objects of art, and, for commercial value, it existed in only limited known quantities.

Flood reflected how the very word *treasure* had fired his own imagination since childhood. It conjured up pictures of booty taken by pirates from Spanish ships, the untold wealth of gold and jewels—in short, the very thing he saw before him at this moment. Yet now, when the dream had become reality, this vast hoard seemed only like so many sacks of heavy metal—nothing more. It might have been rusty railroad spikes for all it thrilled his emotions. Strange. But, like many things in life, the anticipation was better than the reality. Yet this metal could very well be the cause of his death and that of his two companions.

He muscled several of the smaller, stouter bags out of the kiva, looking warily about each time. Then he spread out the gold and silver and jeweled contents, covering several square yards. And that was only about half of the total. The treasure was not composed mostly of coins as he'd envisioned. Instead, there were small gold bars, decorative plates, salt cellars, pitchers, golden chains, figurines, crosses. Many of the coins were hand-minted and of irregular shape. He emptied the rotted hides, piling up the metal in one huge heap. By the time he had finished, the sun was lighting up the opposite cañon wall in a blaze of red and drying up the dampness left from the night's rain.

Flood paused, his back and arm muscles tiring from all the bending and lifting. Breathing deeply, he mopped his face with a shirtsleeve.

He scanned the valley below but saw nothing. Maybe, just maybe, the guide had gone. But they couldn't be that lucky. He returned to the room where Merliss was aiding McGinnis as he sipped some coffee between clenched teeth. He looked up with clear but pain-filled eyes and grunted something.

"What'd he say?"

McGinnis carefully formed his words without moving his jaw. "By all the tortures of the Inquisition, my head is killing me," he croaked.

"Glad to know you're feeling better," Flood remarked, with no trace of a smile. In fact, he was seriously thankful the old man's mind was still clear. "I've never seen such a pile of gold and silver," Flood went on, pouring himself a cup of coffee and picking up a hard biscuit. "But I spread out about half of it for some snapshots."

"Good," she nodded.

But she didn't seem to be in any hurry. She finished feeding her uncle all that he could swallow. The left side of his jaw and face were horribly swollen, and the swelling had descended into his neck. His lean head was all out of proportion. If the wound didn't become infected, however, he would heal. As Flood sopped his dry biscuit in some of the beans Merliss had prepared, he wondered if any of the jaw muscles had been permanently damaged. Whatever the injuries, Flood was grateful that his quick shot from the hip had probably saved the old man's life. Yet, he couldn't avoid a stab of regret that he hadn't been quick-witted enough to draw down on the guide a few seconds earlier. Well, no use dwelling on the past, he thought, straightening up and swigging the last of his coffee.

Merliss got her box camera from her pack. "Let's go," she said, looking to see how many exposures were left.

As they went out, the professor got to his feet and came after them. He mumbled something unintelligible that sounded like one of his famous oaths, but Flood couldn't make it out.

Merliss gasped at the sight of the golden treasure spread out on the flat paving stones. Even though he'd put it there, Flood imagined if one squinted his eyes just so, it would appear the ground was covered with golden aspen leaves in autumn, rather than gold coins.

"Oh, my," she whispered, moving to touch the exquisite jewelry. She picked up a comb and thrust it into the back of her hair where it was tied at the nape of her neck with a piece of ribbon. Then she slipped over her head a necklace that was incised with a delicate *fleur-de-lys* pattern.

"Don't get too carried away." Flood grinned at the rapture in her eyes.

"Oh, my," she repeated, as if unable to get her breath. "Did you ever see anything like this?"

"Saw a stack of gold bars on display at the Carson City mint one time," Flood replied matter-of-factly. "Smelted from ore out of the Black Hills. Supposedly worth two hundred and eighty thousand dollars. But it was like looking at a stack of yellow bricks. It didn't do anything to me in here." He touched his breast.

McGinnis was down on his knees, examining several of the ancient coins. He mumbled something that sounded like "Mesopotamia." Flood knew the old man was absorbing more information from what he was seeing than both he and Merliss put together.

Flood worked the slide of his rifle, and a cartridge popped out of the ejector. He slipped it back into the loading gate and let the hammer down carefully. Then he drew the Bisley model Colt from his holster and made sure it was fully loaded. "I'm going to climb that tower. See if I can get a better view of the cañon. Stay under cover while you look at that stuff."

The other two did not reply, hardly aware of his going.

The two-story, round tower was at the far end of the cave, and he'd been curious about it before. Probably designed as some sort of look-out post. There was one small door on the back side. Unlike the other structures in the cliff dwelling complex, the second floor of this one was reached by an inside ladder, rather than from the outside. The notched log that served as the stairs was still in place, propped in a hole in the ceiling. He carefully tested his weight on it, and it seemed sturdy enough. In a wetter climate, this log, along with the wooden beams that formed the floor above, would have long since rotted. But they still seemed strong. The single upper room was empty. His feet scuffed up thick dust from the floor as he stepped to one of two windows in the circular room. Undoubtedly this must have been a guard tower. From one window he could see a half mile upstream to where the cañon bent. The other window commanded a full view of the cañon just in front and downstream for a mile until the cañon became brush-choked and narrowed down to the small passageway they had hiked through.

He rested the rifle barrel on the waist-high window sill and scanned the entire expanse of red cañon in front of him, a section at a time, examining every rock and shrub. About a third of it was hidden from his sight by trees and willows. But even a close examination revealed nothing that indicated humans had ever passed through. In the absence of wind, the cañon, with its silt-laden stream winding through it, was silent this morning. As he watched, a huge golden eagle soared down below the lip of the deep cañon in the middle distance, then banked away, and flew out of his range of vision.

The ancient Gallina, or Anasazi, people could have held off a sizeable enemy force from here—especially with plenty of water stored in stone tanks and if the grain bins at the back of the cave were full. But these people had vanished within a relatively short period during the time of the crusades in Europe, and no modern scholars knew why. The world was very old and full of mystery, but here, in this desert climate, little physical change had taken place, except the slow workings of wind and water and frost. Compared to geologic nature, man was about as permanent as the fluffy, windborne seeds of the cottonwood trees below him. As he stared out the window, his eyes felt gritty, and fatigue dragged at him. His mind began to wander.

How ironic it was, he thought, that young men all over the country were rushing to volunteer to fight the Spanish in Cuba, and probably only a fraction of those would see combat. Yet, here he was, completely averse to war and violence, caught in a position of having to kill or be killed. How had he come to be in this position? Every choice a man made led on to other choices, and, before he realized it, he'd gone down a road he had no intention of traveling. He had no moral qualms about self-defense. Yet, Christ had taught that, if a man strikes you on one cheek, you are to turn and offer him the other. The day before he'd left Gethsemani, the abbot, when they were in chapter, had talked on this very thing in regard to the monks' forgiveness of one another's faults. Was this to be taken literally? He shifted uneasily. The teaching seemed very clear. But surely it didn't apply when a killer was trying to take your life. Yet Christ had allowed Himself to be crucified when He could have escaped, or crushed His enemies with divine power. But if men practiced this teaching, the world would be overrun with criminals and dictators. Maybe this teaching was only meant to be an ideal—one that few humans could hope to achieve. Again, it seemed to conflict with God's directives in the Old Testament, and even the writings of the early Church fathers. How could he believe in a religion that held two opposing views as equally true? It made no sense.

"Who has known the mind of the Lord, or who has been His counselor?" The quote leaped, unbidden, from the deep recesses of his memory. Where was it mandated that God had to be logical? But, based on the order of things, logic was one of man's tools for separating truth from falsehood. Christ was quoted as saying He hadn't come to destroy the law, but to fulfill it. But hadn't Christ also said He'd come not to bring peace, but the sword? Maybe this was only a prediction of how men would react to His teachings. Nuances of long-dead ancient languages were undoubtedly lost in translation. Flood considered himself a reasonable man, but maybe, intellectually, he was biting off more than he could digest. He sighed and shoved the whole problem aside and looked out the window again. All this would become moot if he died at the hands of Helverson today, in which case he'd have his answer a lot sooner than expected.

From where he stood, he could not see back into the cave below him to his left. But he could hear Merliss talking to her uncle as she snapped photographs of the treasure. As soon as she was finished, he would get them prepared to leave. He felt sure Helverson was still out there some place, but they had to get away from this cave to get some water. Then, if they could reach the horses and pack mules. . . .

As he carefully climbed down the notched ladder, he thought there had to be some roundabout way that pack mules could be brought into this cañon. He doubted this treasure had been carried in here on the backs of the Scots in the 1500s. Probably at that time there had been no boulders wedged tightly into the narrow neck of the cañon. As he stepped out the low doorway of the tower, a rifle cracked, and the Kodak camera exploded from Merliss's hand.

Chapter Eighteen

Ne Me Perdas Illa Die

"Get down!" Flood shouted, throwing himself toward the base of the low retaining wall at the front of the cave.

As three shots exploded from outside, he saw the professor roll, unhurt, into the empty kiva. Two more shots blasted the stillness. Flood pumped two shots over the wall toward the trees where he detected some faint tendrils of smoke. He crawled to the break in the wall and thrust the rifle barrel through. He saw a flash of movement in the foliage and fired again, without apparent effect. He sighted along the octagonal barrel. He saw another movement to the left and fired. His vision was obscured by thick willows. Helverson was apparently trying to work his way around to the side of the cave onto some higher ground where he could get a better shot, or get into the cave.

Merliss wormed her way to Flood's side.

"Are you hit?" he panted.

"No." She was gripping her left hand. "Hit the camera. Sprained my wrist."

Suddenly she had her pocket pistol in hand and fired.

"I thought you didn't know how to shoot," he said.

"How hard can it be? Just point, and pull the trigger," she said, holding the pistol with both hands and firing again, flinching at the explosion.

"Save your ammunition," he cautioned. "Wait until we can see something."

The blast of the last shots racketed back and forth from the rock walls and died away. The shredded silence flowed back in around them, filling all the vacant spaces. Flood could hear nothing but his own harsh breathing. He strained his eyes toward the upper end of the cave.

"Merliss, he could stay out there and snipe at us all day, and a lucky shot or ricochet could get one of us. I have to lure him into the open . . . somehow." He paused, considering his options. To end this, he had to provoke a confrontation. "Let's do this. Get Mac and crawl into that tower. Next time Helverson fires, I'll pretend to be hit and fall. I'm betting he'll eventually come up here to investigate." He slid the stock of the rifle toward her. "Take this. It's easier to aim than a pistol. Just work this slide to cock it. Don't come out or make any noise. As a last resort, use this to protect yourselves if something happens to me."

She nodded.

He crawled over and explained the plan to McGinnis who, although still in pain, seemed to have regained all his mental powers. Then the professor and his niece retreated under cover into the doorway of the stone tower to begin their climb.

Flood drew his Colt and fired three quick shots over the wall. He ducked back, put his hat on his gun barrel, and raised it barely above the parapet. It drew an answering shot, and the hat spun away. Flood gave a choked cry loud enough to be heard and made an obvious show of falling.

"Marc! Marc!" Merliss screamed on cue. "Oh, no!" She threw herself toward him on the ground behind the low wall.

"Good. Now crawl back inside," Flood whispered.

"Let me stay here," she replied, holding the rifle.

"No. Stay under cover. If he should get me, you still have a chance to save yourselves."

She took his whiskery cheeks in her cool palms and kissed him gently. He felt a warm glow as she squirmed away.

Flood got into position to the sound of phony sobbing and snuffling by Merliss. How long would it take the guide to decide it was safe to approach and finish her and McGinnis? Which way would he come? Over the wall? More likely the best approach was from the far end of the cave, the way they'd originally come in.

Lying flat on his stomach behind a pile of collapsed building stones, Flood carefully shifted into position and gripped his Colt. He didn't have long to wait. In less than five minutes he sensed a slight movement, like a shifting shadow. He held his breath, waiting, slitted eyes fixed on the upper end of the cave. Then he saw Helverson cautiously slipping behind a cedar tree and to the edge of a wall. Finally, easing from cover to cover along the tumbled blocks and corners of buildings, Helverson worked closer, holding his Winchester at waist level.

Feigning unconsciousness, Flood watched him come. He gripped his revolver. *Just a little closer . . . a few feet more . . . ,* he thought.

Helverson was in plain sight now, sweeping the area with the rifle barrel, his wary eyes darting here and there.

Suddenly he raised the carbine and took aim at the prostrate Flood. Flood rolled over, aimed, and fired, all in one smooth motion. The bullet struck the trigger guard or receiver of the rifle and ricocheted away. Helverson howled in surprise and pain and dropped the weapon as he dived for cover.

On his knees, Flood fired again, but his shot went wide of the leaping target. Again he fired, clipping the rock near

Helverson's head. He cocked the Colt and squeezed the trigger. The hammer snapped on a spent shell. No time to reload. His heart leaped as he saw Helverson's bleeding hand clawing at his holster. Just as the pistol cleared the holster, Flood bounded frantically over the rocks and kicked Helverson's damaged hand. The heavy handgun went flying end over end.

But Helverson leg-whipped him in the backs of the knees, sending him crashing face first into the stone wall. For a second or two everything in his vision spun as he collapsed sideways. Helverson came up with a fist-size rock in his left hand and swung at him. Flood dodged and rolled to his feet. He sprang out of range, avoiding the débris on the cluttered floor, his chest heaving. Helverson's right hand was bloody and his forefinger bent at an odd angle, apparently broken. Flood circled left, away from the good left hand with the rock.

So it had come down to this—one on one—a monk against a knight for all the gold in the world. It was like some game he would have played as a kid. And, like a kid playing "king of the hill," he let out a wild whoop that tapered off into a chilling, maniacal laugh. The adrenaline was pumping, and he was ready to do battle with this bear of a man.

The grimace of hate and pain never left Helverson's face. He glanced at his revolver that had been kicked fifty feet away.

"Yeah, try for it, damn you!" Flood grated. The concept of forgiving his enemy was the furthest thing from his mind.

They were both unarmed, but they were not equal. Even with a broken index finger, Helverson was bigger, more powerful.

They circled each other. Flood watched his opponent's eyes and saw the fanatical intensity that signaled a potentially super-mortal strength. He dared not close with Helverson, or the big man would crush his ribs and arms like dry sticks. Flood knew he stood no chance in a rough-and-tumble with this man. Instinctively he understood that quickness was his best hope.

The guide opened his left hand and let the rock fall. With a tight smile he reached behind his back and brought out a knife. At the sight of the gleaming blade, Flood groaned inwardly, but didn't change expression. The weapon suddenly reminded him of the forgotten Templar knife he'd found on the train and had been using in camp. Keeping his eyes on his adversary, he squatted and pulled the knife from between the split layers of leather at his boot top.

As he moved left, Flood tripped over some loose stones and caught himself before he fell. Sensing an opening, the big man sprang forward with amazing agility. Flood managed to dodge the downward blow of the knife and regained his balance. But Helverson kept boring in, holding his injured right hand out of the way and sweeping the knife awkwardly with his left. Before Flood realized what was happening, Helverson had maneuvered himself closer to his fallen pistol. Flood found himself wishing Merliss would ignore his instructions and shoot this man. But maybe she had retreated to the second story with the professor for a better defensive position.

Helverson glanced toward the gun on the floor. The second time he looked, Flood stepped in close and slashed downward with his knife, ripping the sleeve and cutting a gash along the forearm. Helverson dropped the knife. Before he could recover, Flood made an underhand slash toward the guide's mid-section. But Helverson, quick for a big man, twisted away as the knife sliced the front of his shirt. He grabbed up a short piece of cedar lying on the rocks and transferred it to his left hand to use as a club. It was clear he wasn't ambidextrous, but when Flood thrust again, Helverson parried with an upward flick of the cedar club, and the knife went spinning away.

Flood backed off, gripping his wrist that had gone numb from the blow. The man had the power of a grizzly. It took several seconds for searing pain to replace the numbness. Anger boiled up inside him as he watched for an opening. He feinted one way. When Helverson reacted, Flood stepped inside the reach of the club and drove a punch to the midsection with his full hundred and sixty pounds behind it. But his fist thudded into the abdomen as into a rubber wall. Then he knew he was trapped, as Helverson merely grunted, locking him in a clinch with those powerful arms. As the vise tightened, he was like a boy in the grasp of a man, and he could do nothing about it. He felt the vertebrae in his back popping as he was yanked face to face with the guide. The breath was being crushed out of him. Flood was momentarily aware of hooded, bloodshot eyes within inches. With his arms pinned, he could do only one thing—he brought up his knee into the taller man's groin. Helverson gasped, and his grip slackened slightly—just enough for Flood to reach back and grab the broken finger, giving it a hard twist. Helverson roared with pain and let go, but clubbed Flood on the side of the head as he backed away. It was like the heavy slap of a bear as everything tilted crazily in Flood's vision for several seconds. He staggered to his left, and the floor of the cave came up to meet his face. He struggled up to his hands and knees, senses reeling. Helverson rushed past him toward the gun on the ground, flinging a spray of blood from the gashed arm.

Just then the blast of gunfire ripped through the cave, and the revolver went skittering away along the stone floor.

Merliss! was Flood's thought.

But the shot came from the wrong end of the cavern. Another muzzle blast made his ears ring.

"Hold it right there!" a strange voice yelled.

A chill went up Flood's sweaty back as he swayed to his feet. Two men moved into his vision, both with drawn revolvers. One of them gestured at the golden spread on the floor.

"Well, isn't this a sight!" another voice from behind him said. Flood turned his head and saw a third gunman climbing over the retaining wall near the tower at the lower end of the cave.

"Who are you?" Flood grated, trying to catch his breath.

"Just three poor travelers who ain't poor no more!" the short, stocky one gloated. "Damn, Kid, this beats train robbin' all to hell!"

"If you two jaspers want to kill each other, I hate to interrupt," the man Flood took as the leader said. "In fact, in a few minutes we might just help you along. But right now I think we'll have you save a little of that energy to do some work loading this gold for us."

"Just who the hell are you?" Flood asked again, when he could think of nothing else to say.

"Part of the Hole-in-the-Wall gang, I'd wager," Helverson said, his voice flat and depressed. "I recognize that one from a wanted flyer . . . Harvey Logan." He pointed.

"I prefer Kid Curry," the identified man said, squaring his sloping shoulders and shoving back the hat to reveal a receding hairline. A bushy black mustache hid his mouth. Flood looked into the liquid brown eyes that were as expressionless as a rattlesnake's.

"As long as we're doing introductions," the leader said, "I'm Elza Lay." In any other setting, Flood would have taken this clean-shaven man for a merchant or businessman. "This

207

is Sam Ketchum. You may have heard of him. No? Well, no matter. Who're you?"

"We don't care if you two are the Sultans of Squat," Ketchum interrupted with a sneer. "We'll just relieve you of this here gold."

"Luckily we heard your gunshots while we were watering our horses a ways upstream and rode down to have a look," Lay continued.

Flood wondered how the gang had gotten their horses into this cañon. If they'd come from upstream, apparently the cañon opened up farther along, at least enough to provide some trails up to the rimrock.

The one named Ketchum came forward and searched them for weapons. "They're clean."

"Check these other rooms," Lay said.

Where were Merliss and McGinnis? Flood hoped they had retreated to the upper story of the tower and were hearing all this. She was armed and just might be his ace in the hole. For several years, Flood had read in the newspapers of the exploits of Butch Cassidy's Wild Bunch, as the papers called them. What rotten luck to encounter them now! Yet, if these outlaws hadn't shown up, he might have come out on the wrong end of this fight and ended up dead. At least now, he had a little more time.

"A man has to play his cards as they fall, and damned if this isn't a royal flush!" Lay said softly, staring at the treasure.

"Nothing in these other rooms but some camp gear," Ketchum said, stepping out of one of the low stone doorways.

"I'll keep an eye on these two. Kid, you and Sam start hauling that stuff to the wall and dumping it over. We'll bring the horses as close as we can and load up."

"Hell, Elza, there's more gold here than we could carry on half a dozen pack mules!" Ketchum said. "And this rotten leather's falling to pieces," he added, taking hold of one of the leather bags.

"We'll take what we can and hide the rest," Lay said. "Fill up your saddlebags, but don't throw out any food or ammunition to do it."

The wind was gusting again, and Flood averted his eyes from the fine grit being whipped into his face. Was it the ghosts of the Anasazi, returning at the sound of gunfire and violence to their ancient stone dwellings? Flood felt a little light-headed, possibly from the blows he'd taken, but the spirit world seemed nearly as relevant as what his senses told him was actually taking place.

Clouds had blocked the sun, and a rumble of thunder sounded in the distance.

"Hurry up with that stuff!" Lay yelled over the wind. "Looks like some weather brewing."

"Damned glad you wanted to head into cañon country," Ketchum panted, a grin fixed to his round face. He piled a blanket to overflowing with gold plates and coins, grasped its corners, and dragged it to the edge of the retaining wall.

"Well, I've got an itchy feeling between my shoulder blades like I get every time a posse's after us. I'd bet they formed up in Trinidad and are hot on our trail right now," Lay said.

"If all this gold slows us down, we'll pitch some of it out," Kid Curry said. "There's plenty more." Even his dour expression had become almost jovial.

"What a predicament, huh, Kid?" Ketchum said, grinning. "We'll never have to pull another job as long as we live."

A shot blasted from Lay's pistol, and Flood started violently.

"Keep your hands where I can see 'em!" the outlaw ordered Helverson. The guide slowly withdrew his hand from inside his jacket.

"My damned finger's busted," Helverson growled, holding up the damaged right hand.

"Kid, come and tie this fella's finger to his hand. Find a stick and put a splint on it. And wrap up that cut on his arm."

"What the hell for?" Kid Curry growled. "So he'll make a better-looking corpse?"

Flood shivered at the words.

"No . . . so he'll be able to work and help us load this gold," Lay replied.

While this rough first aid was being applied, Flood watched Helverson's face. The big man went pale, his lips compressed and beads of sweat formed on his forehead, but he didn't utter a sound as the finger was pulled straight. Flood had to admit the guide had a high tolerance for pain.

Ketchum dumped another load of gold over the low wall and gave a high-pitched laugh as it went crashing in a pile down the slope. "Gaw damn, this is fun!" he chortled.

In spite of Lay's orders, neither of the other two men had gone to get the horses.

"You two get to throwing that gold over the wall!" Lay said, motioning to Flood and Helverson. "Kid, keep 'em covered and make sure they work. I'm going down to bring up the horses so we can get loaded."

Two hours later, Lay rode up, leading the other two horses with empty saddlebags flopping. He'd made three trips up the cañon already, and there appeared to be nearly as big a pile of gold objects and coins as before he'd started. But now it was all in a heap on a sandbar below the cave.

Lay dismounted and surveyed the glowing pile of yellow metal as he shook his head. "Damn, boys, I must be dreaming. This couldn't be happening. We've been working like slaves, and we've still got this much more."

"Where'd you stash the rest of it?" Kid Curry asked.

"Who cares?" Ketchum said. "He can have that. I'll take the rest of this!" He seemed almost giddy.

"Got it in a safe hiding place upcañon a ways," Lay replied cautiously, glancing at Flood and Helverson. He looked at the sky. "Much as I hate to say it, we'll have to leave the rest of this. But the good news is, I think the storm that was dusting up a while ago is moving around to the north of us."

Flood had not been able to retrieve his hat, and the sun, through a thin overcast, was burning his face. While the outlaws talked, he knelt down on one knee in the sand and wiped his face with a shirtsleeve. He thought again of Merliss and McGinnis. She was smart enough to stay under cover. She might even be watching all this from a window in the guard tower. He glanced up casually at the cliff dwelling, but saw no sign of her. She and the wounded professor must be suffering from thirst by now. If it weren't for the silty water in the stream nearby, he certainly would be.

"We gonna spend the night here?" Ketchum asked. "I'm dead tired."

"No. We'll take as much of this as we can carry and ride a few miles out of this cañon before we camp," Lay said.

"What about them?" Ketchum asked, jerking his head at Flood and Helverson.

"We got all the work out of them that we need," Kid Curry said. "Shoot 'em!"

211

Chapter Nineteen

Supplicanti Parce, Deus

A chill went over Flood at the icy manner of Kid Curry. It was no wonder he was known as the tiger of the Wild Bunch.

"Why kill us? You got the gold," he heard himself saying. He hoped it didn't sound like begging, because these men probably respected strength—not weakness.

"Damned good question," Elza Lay said. "We're here for money . . . not murder. Maybe we should leave their guns a little way off and let 'em go t' killing each other like they were doing when we got here."

Ketchum guffawed at this. "Hell, they was doin' all right with fists and clubs. Don't give 'em no guns," he said.

"You let them live and they'll make trouble for us, sure," Kid Curry said.

"Kid, we've got enough charges against us to stretch our necks ten times over," Elza Lay said.

"That's why I think we should finish 'em," Kid Curry growled, scowling and fingering his holstered pistol.

"Robbing is one thing, but outright murder is another," Lay said. "It would just make those damned Pinkertons and marshals more determined. I'm not shooting any unarmed men. It's a matter of pride. And I'm not standing by to watch you do it, either," he added in an ominous tone.

Flood held his breath as the tense silence stretched out between the two. There was a sharp rumble of thunder some-where off to the north, and Flood could see a gray veil of rain in the distance.

"Aren't you the least bit curious as to who these men are and how they happened to be fighting over enough gold to fill the U.S. Treasury? Why don't they just split it? And where are their horses?" Lay looked from Kid Curry to Ketchum. "I was looking at some of those coins," Lay continued. "They're very old, and it's a sure bet they weren't minted by the In-dians. That stuff came from somewhere in Europe, a long time ago."

The stocky Ketchum shrugged. "Never really thought about it. We'll melt it down later. Nobody'll know where it came from."

"I don't care," Kid Curry said. "But you've got a point about not making the law any hotter on us than they already are. We've got the gold now. Let's get out of here. These two won't be going far on foot."

"Then get those saddlebags stuffed and we'll make tracks," Lay replied.

While the other two were engaged at this, Lay stepped over to Flood and Helverson who were sitting on the sand. "You boys want to tell me a little bit about all this?" he asked.

Flood said nothing. Helverson also sat in glum silence.

"Well, suit yourselves. Maybe I ought to let Curry shoot you in the foot to slow you down some in case you have some horses or mules corralled around here some place."

To forestall this idea Flood said: "They're back down-stream a few miles. The cañon's blocked with rocks."

Lay nodded and turned away. "Sam, did they have any food stashed up there that we could use?"

"Hardly any."

"OK. If you're about loaded, let's ride."

"Might save these animals if we walk them," Kid Curry suggested.

"Good idea," Lay agreed. "They'll be hauling a lot of weight today. *Adiós,* gents," Lay said, turning to Flood and Helverson. "If anyone should ask how you were treated by the Hole-in-the-Wall gang, I hope you give us a good recommendation. We didn't harm you in the least, and we left so much gold you couldn't spend it all in a lifetime. Couldn't ask for anything better than that." He gave them a mock salute and, taking the reins of his horse, trudged away with the other two outlaws.

It was nearly a half mile to the first bend in the cañon, and the two men watched silently as the three robbers and their burdened horses grew gradually smaller. Flood was edging away from the big guide, assessing his chances, ready for Helverson to take up where he'd left off.

"Where's McGinnis and the girl?" the guide asked. "They gotta be hid up there some place." He turned to look toward the cliff dwelling. "I heard her scream when you pretended to be hit."

"What if I told you they slipped out and are gone for the horses?" Flood said.

"You'd be lying," he snapped. "They were in that cave . . . at least, the girl was . . . just after sunup. And nobody's come outta there since, or I'd've seen them."

"There's a way out through the back . . . a crack in the rock that leads to the top of the cañon," Flood lied. In case Helverson somehow killed or disabled him, he didn't want the guide going after Merliss and Mac. The treasure had been found, even though more than half of it was now beyond their reach. Helverson would still want to silence him, at least out of spite, somehow blaming Flood and McGinnis for the loss.

"Hell, if there was a way out, you'd have taken it, too," the guide said.

Helverson's broken finger had been splinted with a short stick and wrapped, bound to the middle finger. The right hand could be used with the left to pick up large objects but wasn't good for much else. Helverson was considerably handicapped, at least by the pain, and the big man's energy seemed to be seriously depleted. His shoulders sagged as they watched the outlaws pass beyond a stand of willows and out of sight.

Then Helverson turned toward him, and Flood saw a look he'd never seen before. When they'd faced off in the cavern, Helverson had shown a cold, calculating ferocity. Then it had not been personal—merely professional. But now the big man's sun-blistered face was twisted with hate. Flood saw the jaw muscles twitching and felt the hooded eyes boring into him with a piercing intensity. Sudden fear stabbed his gut.

Helverson sprang at him with a roar like a grizzly. Tired as he was, Flood had a burst of adrenaline and leaped out of the way. Helverson was agile and energized with fury, but Flood was quicker. Blind rage was to Flood's advantage; he was able to slip and dodge the bull-like rushes.

It seemed an endless stretch of time but was probably no more than five minutes that Helverson kept coming and Flood kept dodging, now and then taking a glancing blow, or getting in a stiff jab, trying to stay out of the guide's reach. In the windless cañon with the sun boring down, sweat was stinging his eyes. From exertion and lack of food and sleep, Flood could feel his strength ebbing. His breath came in great, sobbing gasps.

He finally saw some sign that the big man was also tiring. Helverson was not made of rubber and piano wire, after all. The guide paused, chest heaving, blood running from his nose where one of Flood's sharp jabs had connected. He glared at Flood as if lining him up in his sights for one final rush. Flood sensed what was coming and sidled to his right to keep his back away from the stream. Helverson wiped his nose with the back of his hand, smearing blood across his cheek.

Flood was conscious of a dull, rushing sound and hoped he wasn't about to pass out. He was swaying on his feet from sheer exhaustion. But the faint sound began to grow louder, rising to a low roar, and he suddenly realized it was not inside his head. He turned to look up the cañon and saw something that appeared, from a distance, like huge, white snakes writhing along the cañon floor. He opened his mouth to say something, but what came out was a grunt as Helverson's shoulder slammed into his mid-section. The sloping sandbar was all that saved him from broken ribs as the big man drove him down. The wind was knocked out of him as Helverson leaped astride and began pounding his head with a huge left fist. Flood twisted this way and that, fending off some of the blows with his forearms, but could feel smashing pain as each blow landed. He fought to retain consciousness and breathe as the knuckles bounced off his skull.

Through the descending red veil, he sensed if he didn't escape now, it was all over. He tensed and made one desperate lunge. Helverson, who outweighed him by forty pounds, was caught by surprise and thrown sideways. Flood scrambled away on his hands and knees, a roaring in his ears.

Suddenly a sheet of creamy, brownish water came hissing across the sand, foaming several inches deep around his arms and legs. He looked up. Thundering toward them, about sixty feet away, came a solid wall of water at least seven feet high and nearly vertical. Flood sprang to his feet and ran for his life, forgetting Helverson, while water roared down on them like an avalanche. He bounded through the shallow water and up a slope into a stand of willows. The terrifying roar grew louder behind him, grinding rocks and ripping up small trees. Water was suddenly up to his knees. He leaped up the steeper grade, digging frantically with hands and feet.

Above the roaring, he heard the crack of a rifle. Out of the corner of his eye he saw Helverson falter. Flood snapped his head around as the rifle exploded again and saw the raging brown torrent engulf the big man, whirling him away like a piece of driftwood. There was no point in stopping. The guide was gone.

Then Flood was above it, climbing the tumbled boulders the last hundred feet to the cliff dwelling. He looked back but saw no sign of Helverson in the foaming power of the greenish-brown current. Lungs burning, he finally staggered into the cavern, near collapse. Merliss came running toward him. McGinnis followed slowly behind her, carrying the rifle. Dripping blood and water, Flood hugged her, feeling his heart thudding like it was going to burst.

"Was that you . . . who shot Helverson?" he gasped in her ear.

"No. Uncle Mac fired at him."

"I was aiming at his chest, but I hit him in the leg!" the professor snorted in disgust as he came up.

"Doesn't matter," Flood said, releasing Merliss. "He fell back into the water and got swept away."

"I saw," she nodded.

"Play with fire and you get burned," McGinnis snapped, with no sign of remorse as he fingered the wound on his jaw.

For a minute they stood in silence, staring in stunned fascination at the flash flood. The water, rising fast, had already inundated the sandbars and was sweeping everything before it. The bending willows were barely visible above the surface.

"Will it reach the cave?" Merliss asked.

"I doubt it," Flood said. "This cliff dwelling has been here hundreds of years, and there's no sign of high-water marks on these buildings. And those big cottonwoods just below us are too tough and well-anchored to be undercut or ripped out by this flood, bad as it is."

"A mighty downpour up north of us," McGinnis muttered through his swollen jaw. "Look there," he added, pointing at two saddle horses being swirled, kicking and struggling, in the current.

"Two of the outlaws' horses," Flood nodded. "I don't see any sign of the men." He wondered about their fate. But his mind was dulled, unable to feel any emotion except relief.

They continued to stare at the rumbling river. It had freed them and imprisoned them at the same time. All human danger had been eliminated, but now they were marooned in this cave until the water receded.

As the water rose and filled the cañon from side to side, Flood's adrenaline ebbed, and he began to feel every bruise and cut on his body. His big muscles were already beginning to stiffen.

Merliss was first to shake off their collective shock. "Marc, you're hurt." She touched his face, and he winced at the abrasion on his cheek bone. "Let me clean up those cuts," she said, taking his arm.

"I don't think anything's broken, and my brain seems to be intact," he managed to grin. As she led him away, his eyes fell on the dull gleam of a knife blade. He stooped to pick it up. Except for the lack of rust on the blade and a small crack in the handle, it was nearly identical to the knife that had been clubbed from his hand during the earlier fight. The yellowed ivory grip was carved with the figures of two men riding double on a horse.

"The Templar symbol," Merliss mused. "If there was any doubt about Helverson before, that eliminates it."

Flood took a deep breath, feeling the pain in his ribs. "If I can find the one I dropped, they'll make a nice pair of steak knives."

"I'll stir up the fire," she said. "Looks like we'll be here a few days, and we're almost out of food and water."

Chapter Twenty

Agnus Dei, Qui Tollis Peccata Mundi: Dona Eis Requiem

"By the River Styx, that quicksand swallowed the gold," McGinnis lamented three days later as the three of them walked along the edge of the receding river.

"It might all be piled up downstream at that choke stone," Flood said.

"Not much chance of that," McGinnis replied. "I was stuck in that quicksand, and it's like wet cement. There're big stretches of it all along here," he said, probing with a willow pole. "And, as heavy as that gold is, once it goes down in there, it's not going to be washed back up."

Flood was able to understand his words much better since the swelling in the professor's jaw had shrunk by at least half. Flood thought about the gold and felt sick. But he had to admit that McGinnis was probably right.

"I just hope our horses and mules are safe," Merliss said.

"Helverson was careful about leaving them on high ground," Flood said. "I don't think the water could have reached them."

It was as much wishful thinking as confidence. If the horses were gone or drowned, it was going to be a long, hungry walk back to Santa Fé. But he kept his concerns to himself as he led the way, sometimes having to wade, knee-deep in the muddy water. Each of them carried a willow staff to probe the bottom ahead for unseen drop-offs or quicksand.

They had briefly considered hiking upstream a mile or so to see if they could find any trace of the gold Elza Lay had stashed somewhere in the cañon. But they'd been on survival rations for three days and now were down to nothing but river water that they'd let stand overnight to settle out the silt. Getting to their horses and cached food was imperative. They could come back and search for the gold later when they'd resupplied themselves, and the area had dried up. After seeing two of the outlaws' horses swept away, Flood was doubtful that the three men had escaped with any of the treasure, or even with their lives.

They were more than a half mile from the Stone Castle when Flood looked back at the ancient cliff dwelling. He wondered what other violence those stone rooms might have witnessed over the centuries. Even if he never saw it again, he would never forget this place. And the hooded eyes of Helverson would probably haunt his dreams for months to come. Could the wounded guide have somehow survived this devastation of nature? Highly unlikely. Helverson was tough, but he wasn't superhuman. Flood took a deep breath and turned his back on the silent buildings in the gash of the cliff.

They'd hiked another half mile and had just turned the bend in the cañon that hid the Stone Castle from view when McGinnis stopped Flood with a sharp oath.

"By the touch of King Midas! Look at this!"

Flood and Merliss saw him on his knees at the edge of the muddy stream, digging at something half buried in the wet sand. He sluiced the object around in the water and held it up. The morning sun flashed from an exquisite gold chalice. It was ornately engraved and studded around its stem with small rubies. He set it aside and began looking around. "Maybe there's more."

Instead of helping with the search, Flood went over and picked up the cup. The craftsmanship was superb. On the round, wide base of the chalice were carved, in relief, four figures. From what he could read of the Latin, they represented the four Evangelists: Matthew, Mark, Luke, and John. As he stared at the relic, he thought of how odd it was that one single gold object could hold his attention and interest more than a huge pile of gold coins and works of art. *Man is certainly a strange creature,* he thought, setting the cup back on the sand.

McGinnis hunted for twenty minutes, but found nothing else.

"That was just a fluke, Uncle Mac," Merliss said. "You could hunt for days, and not find any more."

"Then, again, I might find a fortune in the next few minutes," he retorted, eyes on the sandy loam, scuffing his toes here and there. "Whoa!" He jumped back and gave the stream a wide berth. "Quicksand," he explained when they looked at him.

"You scared me," Merliss said with relief. "I thought you saw a snake."

"Well, at least three pieces of the treasure survived," Flood said, indicating the gold necklace and comb Merliss had tried on the day after the discovery and had never taken off.

"That's right. Maybe I'll get to keep these." She looked at her uncle.

"Of course, my dear," he replied with unusual gentleness. "I've got a chalice that predates Charlemagne. And I've also got this." He pulled a gold coin from his pocket. "I'd forgotten I had it."

"Too bad you won't be able to prove you've found a treasure with just those four items," Flood said, wondering if he could have somehow done anything different to prevent the loss.

"We do have one thing," Merliss said thoughtfully. She reached into her nearly empty pack and held up a roll of film. "I'd just taken the last shot and cranked off the end of the roll when that bullet hit the camera. My Kodak was ruined, but the film wasn't exposed."

Flood grinned. "You're a wonder to even think of such a thing after nearly getting your hand shot off. If those pictures come out, you'll at least have a photographic record in black and white of our find."

"Unfortunately, archaeologists are a skeptical bunch on the whole," McGinnis said sadly, shaking his white head. "Photographs can be faked, and I'm afraid most of my colleagues will think it's only a pile of costume jewelry and lead slugs. Nothing will convince the academic world except producing the bulk of the treasure."

"I'm sorry the way things turned out," Flood said with genuine regret. "I didn't figure to share in any of that wealth, but I know just finding it meant everything to you and your reputation."

"Don't give it a thought, laddy. You did your best. It was an act of God. I'm a lot further ahead than when I started this jaunt. And if it weren't for you, I'd be lying dead back there with a bullet in my brain."

Flood looked at the scabbing wound along the professor's jaw line; it was healing nicely. His face was returning to normal size even though McGinnis complained that he thought his jaw had been knocked out of line.

"We'll get re-outfitted in Santa Fé and go back and search the upper part of that gorge for half the treasure the Hole-in-the-Wall gang stashed," Flood said hopefully.

Shortly after, they reached the narrowest part of the

cañon. Seeing no sign of rain clouds in the distance, they waded, hip-deep, through the cut. To their surprise, the huge choke stones that had plugged the bottleneck had been blasted out by the force of the water. By early afternoon they reached the high benchland where they'd left their animals. From the height of the snagged driftwood, they saw where the flood had come within ten feet of the stone corral. But the animals were safe, although somewhat lean.

Their remaining food and ammunition were also untouched and dry beneath the rock overhang in the cañon wall.

After hobbling the animals on better grass, Flood gathered some dry driftwood and built a fire. McGinnis and Merliss dug out bacon, canned beans, and flour for biscuits. It was a feast none of them would have traded for the treasure.

"Well, are you sorry it's over?" Flood asked Merliss as they sat, side by side, pleasantly stuffed, staring into the flames. Long afternoon shadows crept down the cañon.

"It's not over," she replied. "We don't know if Helverson's dead. We don't know if the gang got away with half the treasure. We don't know if any of the Templars will find out about all this, try to retrieve the lost gold, or try to take revenge on Uncle Mac." She turned her blue eyes on him. "I know one thing . . . whatever I do from here on, my life will never be the same again. What about you?"

"Beyond immediate survival, I haven't given a thought to what I'll do next," he replied truthfully. "I have only two goals . . . one is to resolve a conflict in my personal faith."

"What's that?" she asked.

"You may consider it a tempest in a teapot when I tell you," he said with a touch of embarrassment. "Why don't you let me buy you a steak dinner in Santa Fé and we'll discuss it?"

224

"It's a date," she replied, slipping her hand into his. "You know," she continued, regarding him with a penetrating gaze, "men generally tend to tie themselves in knots arguing points of religion and philosophy . . . abstract things, mostly." She smiled. "Now, women, on the other hand, are much more practical and down-to-earth. But men and women are just two sides to one coin. Both necessary to human commerce, you might say. So, I'm sure there's a practical solution, if not a logical one, to whatever's bothering you."

"You sound like a teacher," he said, marveling at her insight. Her words were reassuring, rather than belittling or sarcastic.

As if his life were rotating into focus, he began to see that leaving the monastery was not the failure he'd first supposed. Many men tried the contemplative life, but only a few found it their true calling. From past experience he'd found that apparent blind alleys usually contained some hidden escape route. Through the crack of the hidden gate Merliss seemed to be opening, he thought he could glimpse a positive future—possibly for both of them.

He didn't know how she viewed the loss of the gold, but, ironically, he felt stronger for it, almost as if the crushing burden of impending wealth and fame had fallen from his shoulders.

"And what's the second goal you mentioned?" she asked.

"To see you a lot more often than just at one steak dinner."

Her color seemed to rise slightly in the firelight, but she met his gaze frankly. "I think that goal can be accomplished without too much trouble," she smiled.

From the other side of the fire came the gentle sounds of the professor's snoring.

Epilogue

Professor Roddy McGinnis, Marcus Flood, and Merliss McGinnis spent the remainder of that summer and four succeeding summers searching for the treasure, but came away empty-handed. The professor made another six trips, each time with three or four student helpers, but nothing of the treasure was ever found. As far as anyone knows, it remains buried deep in quicksand along the bottom of a remote cañon in northern New Mexico.

Two days after the flood, the three members of the Hole-in-the-Wall gang were found afoot on the barren rimrock by a pursuing posse. A furious gun battle ensued. Three of the posse were killed, and Sam Ketchum was so severely wounded in the arm that Elza Lay and Kid Curry were forced to leave him behind when they managed to steal two of the law men's horses and escape. Before he died a week later of blood poisoning, Ketchum raved about a lost golden treasure. The authorities assumed he was delirious.

Elza Lay, recovering from wounds, was captured a month later, tried, and sentenced to life in prison. However, he was released in 1906 and went straight for the remainder of his days, dying in 1934. Harvey Logan, alias Kid Curry, was killed during a robbery attempt in 1903.

In 1908, Professor McGinnis found a partial human skeleton that was still wearing one leather boot that belonged to Dan Helverson. McGinnis wasted no time collecting the bones in a flour sack, adding some rocks, and sinking it all in a bed of quicksand. Helverson was only one of several hundred persons in the United States who went missing during that year of 1898. Since he had no family, his disappearance was never pursued.

As time went on, the professor's behavior became so erratic and unpredictable that the University of Chicago forced him into retirement in 1911. Since no treasure turned up, Helverson had vanished, and Professor McGinnis never publicized his discovery of the golden hoard, the ruling council of the Western Knights Templar decided the whole thing had been a hoax, ceased pursuing Roddy McGinnis, and spared the life of the Grand Master, Thomas D'Arcy.

Marcus Flood married Merliss McGinnis in 1899 and eventually became a director of the Museum of Natural History in Louisville, Kentucky where he remained for twenty-two years. He continued to make retreats to the Trappist monastery at Gethsemani on a regular basis for the rest of his life, but never fully resolved the moral conflict that had driven him from the monastery. The question of aggression versus forgiveness was one that had perplexed generations of greater minds than his.

In accordance with the Last Will and Testament of Roddy McGinnis, the diary of Peter Stirling was published in 1921. Included in the same volume was a first-hand account by Mrs. Merliss McGinnis Flood of the abortive treasure hunt, supported by black and white photographs that purported to be of the treasure itself. The book was a bestseller for nearly a year, until scholars dismissed it as a clever fraud.

One man, however, was convinced of its authenticity. Eighty-three-year-old Thomas D'Arcy, retired vice president of the Union Pacific Railroad and former Grand Master of the Western Knights Templar. However, D'Arcy had become increasingly senile. The current Grand Master politely, but firmly, told the old man the diary was no more genuine than the fabled Seven Cities of Gold of Spanish times because scientists had already excavated every cliff dwelling in northwestern New Mexico and had found not the first item of gold.

The ancient gold chalice willed to St. Bridget of Erin church in Chicago is still in use at special Masses. Merliss McGinnis Flood wore the gold necklace with the *fleur-de-lys* design and the decorative comb for years before passing them on to her daughter when she came of age. It is unknown if the Western Knights Templar are still pursuing their ambitious goal of establishing a New Holy Roman Empire.

About the Author

Tim Champlin, born John Michael Champlin in Fargo, North Dakota, was graduated from Middle Tennessee State University and earned a Master's degree from Peabody College in Nashville, Tennessee. Beginning his career as an author of the Western story with SUMMER OF THE SIOUX in 1982, the American West represents for him "a huge, ever-changing block of space and time in which an individual had more freedom than the average person has today. For those brave, and sometimes desperate souls who ventured West looking for a better life, it must have been an exciting time to be alive." Champlin has achieved a notable stature in being able to capture that time in complex, often exciting, and historically accurate fictional narratives. He is the author of two series of Westerns novels, one concerned with Matt Tierney who comes of age in SUMMER OF THE SIOUX and who begins his professional career as a reporter for the Chicago *Times-Herald* covering an expeditionary force venturing into the Big Horn country and the Yellowstone, and one with Jay McGraw, a callow youth who is plunged into outlawry at the beginning of COLT LIGHTNING. There are six books in the Matt Tierney series and with DEADLY SEASON a fifth featuring Jay McGraw. In THE LAST CAMPAIGN, Champlin provides a compelling narrative of Geronimo's last days as a renegade leader. SWIFT THUNDER is an exciting and compelling story of the Pony Express. In all of Champlin's stories there are always unconventional plot ingredients, striking historical details, vivid characterizations of the multitude of ethnic and cultural diversity found on the frontier, and narratives rich and original and surprising. His exuberant tapestries include lumber schooners sailing the West Coast, early-day wet-plate photography, daredevils who thrill crowds with gas balloons and the first parachutes, tong wars in San Francisco's Chinatown, Basque sheepherders, and the *Penitentes* of the Southwest, and are always highly entertaining. A TRAIL TO WOUNDED KNEE is his next **Five Star Western**.